MINERVA CLARK

gets a clue

Minerva Clark

gets a clue

BY Karen Karbo

SCHOLASTIC INC.

New York Toronto London Auckland Sydney
Mexico City New Delhi Hong Kong Buenos Aires

ISBN-13: 978-0-439-93419-0
ISBN-10: 0-439-93419-2

12 11 10 9 8 7 6 5 4 3 2 1   7 8 9 10 11 12/0

Printed in the U.S.A.   40

First Scholastic printing, February 2007

For Fiona,
perfect just the way she is

- 1 -

THe WORST DaY OF MY LiFe began at the video arcade. It was a teacher-planning day, so there was no school. I didn't want to go to Tilt, but Quills wanted me to go with him, so I said yes. It was before my accident, when I said yes a lot, even when I wanted to say no.

I have three older brothers. Each one is two years, two months, and two days younger than the one before him. Weird, huh? Quills was twenty-two and was on the verge of graduating from college. He was the BIC that day, the Brother-in-Charge.

The worst day of my life was also the longest day of my life, but isn't that how it always works?

Quills had the day off from Kinko's, where he worked making sure the good people of the world got their flyers

1

Xeroxed, but he's really the bass guitarist for the band Humongous Bag of Cashews. He's not famous yet, but one day he will be. In the meantime, he dyes his hair crayon yellow and says things like "the good people of the world," which is how famous people talk. His real name is Michael.

I so did not want to go to Tilt. I secretly thought it was stupid and boring. And because it was next to the movie theater, it always smelled like stale popcorn and bathroom cleaner. At Tilt I would do nothing but stand there and watch Quills and his best friend, Toc, who was meeting us there, play Police 911 and Star Trek Voyager for about eight hundred hours.

I could have just said I wanted to stay home and work on my book of rebuses (here's my new one:

$$YY + AM + \text{👁}$$

Too wise am I. Get it?) and play with my ferret, Jupiter, but if it got around school that I wanted to stay home instead of go to Tilt, people like Hannah McAdams, who was supposed to be my best friend, would call me a freak show loser.

Hannah and I have known each other since Little Acorns Preschool, when we had both loved digging in the dirt with teaspoons in search of buried treasure. One time we found a Susan B. Anthony dollar, which I still have, and once we found an old piece of tire we were convinced was an Indian arrowhead. Hannah was the first person not in my family to spend the night at my house and the first girl who was allowed to go on vacation with us one year to a dude ranch in California, where she fell off an old pale yellow palomino named Popcorn that was just standing there nibbling on some grass. Once, in third grade, it looked as if we would not be best friends anymore—a girl named Summer Walters slept over at Hannah's house more than I did—but then Summer moved to Florida when her mother got transferred.

Hannah says she never called me a freak show loser, but I have the note from Julia, another girl in the seventh grade, to prove she did. If you believe Julia. Which maybe you shouldn't. I don't know.

Anyway, if it got out that I secretly thought Tilt was stupid and boring, and if you believe that Hannah *did* call me a freak show loser, she would probably call me a double freak show loser, and I would probably run to the girls' room and cry, and then a rumor would start that I was bulimic, and then people would say double freak show loser doesn't even *begin* to describe what's wrong with Minerva Clark, because how could I be bulimic and still have fat legs?

So I put on my favorite too-big khaki pants and my

favorite red Vans hoodie and crawled into the backseat of the Electric Matador, a metallic-blue car from the 1970s that was hideously old and ugly. To make matters worse, Quills had a pair of bullhorns strapped to the front. I didn't know why Quills couldn't have a normal beige Honda that people didn't stare at.

The backseat was full of old music magazines and computer parts and empty Mountain Dew cans. It was like the nest of some big weird bird. I liked to sit in the backseat, even if no one was up front, so I could duck if I saw anybody I knew.

On the way to Tilt, Quills passed me his cell phone so I could call my friend Reggie. Reggie and I have known each other even longer than Hannah and I have known each other. We've known each other since whatever people are before they're actual babies, because Reggie's mom and my mom took prenatal water aerobics together at the YMCA. Even though Hannah McAdams is my official best friend, Reggie is my secret best friend. Because he's a boy he obviously can't be my official best friend. Sometimes I really hate seventh grade.

"Hey, Reg, it's me. Wanna meet me at Tilt? Quills and me are headed there now."

"My mom wants me to go shoe shopping. I'd rather chew on a lightbulb," he said.

"And then mash the leftovers into your eyes," I said. We said stuff like this all the time. I would never suggest that Hannah McAdams mash a broken lightbulb into her eyes.

"I got ahold of my bro's Boston Tea Party report," said Reggie. "We can recycle it for Hazelnut's class." Hazelnut was Ms. Hazelton, our social studies teacher.

"Didn't your brother have Hazelnut, too?" I asked.

"About a hundred years ago."

"I don't know," I said. That morning I was still the kind of girl who didn't like to get in trouble, who didn't like anything that drew attention to herself.

"I'll flashy thing her and she won't remember."

Reggie was a huge fan of the movie *Men in Black*. Or, as one of our favorite rebuses went:

BLmenACK

Reggie spent a lot of time on the Internet trying to find our if the technology to make the memory eraser really existed. He wanted to use it to erase the memories of everyone who thought he was a pathetic geek instead of the cool geek he wanted to be.

Reggie was already at Tilt when Quills and I arrived. He was eating a soft pretzel. Reggie had thick brown hair that sometimes got bigger than mine and really long

eyelashes. Ladies stopped Reggie on the street sometimes and told him how lucky he was, having eyelashes
like that. Like every other boy in my class, he was about
two feet tall. I towered over Reggie. I was Gigantor next
to him. Even though I didn't think he was hot or
anything, it was still depressing.

Reggie raised his pretzel in salute.

We went inside. Quills scooted over and grabbed an
empty game before anyone else nabbed it. Quills's best
friend, Toc, stood in front of one of the change machines
against the wall. He wore his black hair in a tiny ponytail
high on top of his head, like someone in an old Japanese
painting, and in the summer he painted his toenails blue.
Toc was the lead singer and founding member of
Humongous Bag of Cashews. Toc stood for The Original Cashew, but his real name was Brad. Last year,
in sixth grade, when one of our spelling words was
"flamboyant," I wrote, "My brother's friend Toc is
flamboyant."

"Incoming nefarious activity," Toc announced loudly.

I pretended I knew what that meant. Probably something a little creepy, knowing Toc.

He handed Reggie and me each a five-dollar bill,
except the paper felt funny and ordinary, not crinkly and
important. I didn't need to look close to know the bill
was a color Xerox.

"You gotta make sure you use this one," said Toc. He stood in front of the last machine in the row.

"Why?" said Reggie, turning the bill over in his hand.

"Said nefarious activity only works on old machines. The new ones got special high-tech sensors or something."

Toc took the fake bill he'd given me and slid it into the machine. It clanked twice, then spat out some coins, filling the tiny metal cup beneath its plastic flap with quarters.

"Sweet!" said Reggie.

I remembered then that Reggie liked to call Toc a poseur. Secretly, I think Reggie thought Toc was cool. Toc had a motorcycle and a Fender guitar.

"Isn't that illegal or something?" I asked.

"Not 'or something.' It's totally illegal," he said. He collected the quarters, stuck out his tongue, bugged out his dark eyes, and strolled off to find Quills. Toc was so irritating. I didn't know how Quills could be best friends with him. Probably they dug in the dirt together in preschool.

Reggie was staring over my shoulder at something. I turned to follow his gaze and saw the arcade game I despised more than any other: Dance Dance Revolution.

Crap.

I wasn't supposed to say that word, even though it wasn't a true swear word.

A feeling of doom came over me. Reggie love love *loved* DDR. I'd forgotten Tilt had one. Had I remembered, I'd have stayed home and worked on my rebuses and let everyone and his brother think I was a double freak show loser.

Two guys with wispy mustaches were already on the dance pad, stomping around like madmen. The techno music blared, and the pink and blue arrows blinked on the metal dance pad. Reggie watched the arrow on the screen. He tapped his foot and played air drums. I should have made a beeline to the exit.

Sometimes I am so lame.

Reggie saw the look on my face.

"You are such a wuss," he said.

I could feel my cheeks heat up, like there was a little campfire burning inside each one. "I am not."

"We can put it on light difficulty."

I didn't say anything.

"You're turning into one of those girly girls who doesn't want to get her hair messed up."

"That is so not true!" I said. Of course it was true. I didn't want to get my hair messed up. I'd spent twenty minutes in front of the bathroom mirror that morning patting on something I'd bought at Rite Aid with my babysitting money, a green serum with the consistency of snot, which was supposed to get rid of my frizzies.

The wispy mustache guys finished their game and left. Reggie hopped on the dance pad and started feeding quarters into the machine. This was so easy for him. He was short and quick. He did not have feet so big people made jokes about how somewhere a circus clown was missing his shoes.

I stepped onto the pad, positioned my feet on the arrows, and knew I'd made a big mistake. I'd forgotten I'd worn the biggest boats I owned. My purple Chuck Taylors were lost somewhere in my room, so I'd grabbed a pair of gigantic white Nikes.

There was one other thing. Quills had told me to leave my ferret, Jupiter, at home. But there was no way. Ferrets are creatures who like companionship. I take Jupiter everywhere I go, except to school. Most of the time, he just sleeps in the pocket of my hoodie. He was asleep now, but he wouldn't be for long.

The music started. It beeped and bleated and Reggie stepped and stomped. I tried to follow the arrows on the screen telling me where to put my feet, but every time I moved I stepped on my own toe.

Then Jupiter woke up with a start. I had to squeeze both sides of my pouch shut so he wouldn't escape.

He didn't like that. He leaped around inside my pocket.

I started sweating. I could smell my BO. I had been so busy with the green anti-frizz serum that I'd forgotten to put on deodorant. How stupid could I be?

Out of the corner of my eye I saw a flash of red and blue, people entering the arcade. They stopped behind me and Reggie to watch. I could hear them talking, laughing. I knew if I turned to look I would get farther behind in my steps. I tried to concentrate on the flashing arrows and bounce along with the music. I couldn't help it. I turned right around and there were Julia and the two Chelseas.

When Hannah and I were in a fight, she sometimes hung out with Julia at lunchtime, but that was only if one of the Chelseas was absent. Chelsea Evans was lactose intolerant and was always in the nurse's office with a stomachache, and Chelsea de Guzman's parents took her out of school a lot to go on fancy vacations to places like Prague and Aspen. They were the ones who started calling me Gigantor. The Chelseas that is, not Chelsea de Guzman's parents.

They'd stopped at DDR to watch the show. I heard giggling as I clomped around. Why didn't I just stop? I knew I should have told Reggie no. I knew I should have told Quills no. I hated how I always said yes when I didn't want to.

Then I heard one of them say the word "spaz."

I felt both pitted-out sweaty and like I was going to cry. The pink and blue arrows got blurry. The music pounded in my head. I lost my balance and crashed into Reggie. He didn't miss a beat. The giggles behind me turned to snorting laughter, the kind that makes you laugh even harder.

That's when I missed a step and the edge of my foot landed on the edge of the dance pad, my ankle twisted, and I fell off. Jupiter was thrashing around my pocket. I worried about squishing him, so I turned as I fell and landed on my back, right onto the dirty, fried-food smelling carpet. My head went *clunk!* I'd knocked the wind out of myself.

I looked up into the faces of Julia and the Chelseas. Their straight swingy hair hung like show dog ears on either side of their skinny heads. I would never have that hair. Julia and Chelsea Evans had their hands clamped to their mouths, but I could still see their smiles. Chelsea de Guzman was madly text messaging someone.

Julia squeaked, "Oh my God, are you all right?"

They all burst out laughing. Reggie kept on stomping around on the dance pad.

I caught my breath, rolled over onto my knees, and got on all fours. I was face-to-face with the egg-smooth knees of Chelsea de Guzman, who was wearing a stone-washed jean miniskirt. Her knees wobbled around as she shrieked with laughter. It was the hysteria that kicks in when you start laughing so hard because you are laughing so hard. I got to my knees, brushed the ancient food crumbs and gunk from the bottom of a thousand shoes off my palms. Reggie was deep into his madman dance, his thick brown bangs bouncing off his shiny-with-sweat forehead. He would not help me. Quills and Toc would not help me.

I lurched to my feet and ran out of Tilt, past the movie theater, past Sbarro's and Chicken Connection and McDonald's Express, and down the long corridor that led to the bathrooms. No one was there. I locked myself in one of the stalls but didn't even pretend to go to the bathroom. For some reason I remembered last year's talent show. Quills had convinced me to sing "I Wanna Be Sedated" by the Ramones, and an eighth-grade boy yelled out, "*We* want you to be sedated," and everyone laughed so hard it made me forget the words, and I just stood up there with the campfires blazing in my cheeks.

I sat on the toilet in my stall for what seemed like eight hundred years, sobbing like some stupid baby. Ladies came in and out, but no one noticed me at all. I tried to pull out a piece of toilet paper to blow my nose, but it was a fat roll crammed into its holder and all I could rip off were scraps.

Was this what my entire life was going to be like? Or was this simply what happened on the worst day of your life?

If this sort of thing happened to Julia, the two Chelseas, Hannah, or Reggie, I never saw it. They had small bodies that were easy to control. They had normal-sized feet. Even Reggie's head of springy brown hair wasn't like mine—a thick snarl that was curly in front, wavy on the sides, and straight in back. My hair could be the monster in a sci-fi movie.

I reached inside the pouch of my hoodie to pet Jupiter. Once on Animal Planet I saw a show about ferrets and how they can sense a person's feelings. Jupiter probably would have rather been dashing around playing, but he stretched out flat along the bottom of my pouch so I could run my hand over his soft white fur, trying to calm myself down.

Then I walked around the mall for a while, half waiting for Reggie to realize that I wasn't coming back to Tilt. I thought as my secret best friend he would come in search of me. Quills would kill me for leaving Tilt without telling him, but I didn't even care. I found a dollar on the ground and bought myself an Orange

Julius, stuck my snarly hair inside my hood, and started walking home.

While I was walking, I thought up a new rebus.

DKI

Mixed-up kid. I thought it wasn't bad.

-2-

I HAD WALKED ABOUT SIX blocks when I heard a car zoom past. It was one of those wild spring Portland days where it rains really hard for about three minutes, then the sun comes out. The car stopped at the corner and waited. It was a red Jetta, and it was jacked up just a little in the back, kind of perky. On a normal day, a day that was not the worst day of your life, getting a ride in the rain would be a most excellent thing. Today, though, it was another of the strange, upsetting things that would happen.

Although I didn't recognize the car, I knew right away it must be my cousin Jordan, on account of the bumper sticker: BLOND IF YOU'RE HONK. Ha ha ha. Everyone knew Jordan got the best grades in the entire world. She got higher than straight A's. (How is that even possible?) She had straight light brown hair—the kind that turns blond in the summertime—and played lacrosse, that sport where you wear a plaid skirt. She was perfect. She had been my favorite cousin since the day at Little Acorns Preschool when I learned what the word meant. Jordan never had a zit that I saw or got food stuck in her teeth. She was girly in a good way. She wore pink T-shirts sometimes, but she didn't have a fit if a spider showed up in the kitchen. In the last year my feelings for her had gotten more complicated, like everything in my life. On the days I didn't want to be her, I hated her for her perfection.

At the time I didn't wonder where Jordan had gotten the red Jetta. Later, I would wonder about it a lot.

She tooted the horn, and I walked across the wet grass on the parking strip and opened the car door. Jupiter had fallen back asleep, making me look as if I had a big, middle-aged man stomach roll. I didn't care. Well, actually, I did care, but not enough to wake Jupiter up and take him out.

Jordan was on her cell. She waved me inside the car. Her cheeks were blotchy red and she was madly finger-ing one of her big hoop earrings, the kind I'd love to wear but am too young for, like I am for all the good stuff.

As I slid into the Jetta, Jordan said, "Dude, what part

of 'not interested' don't you understand?" She snapped the phone closed and dropped it on the hump between the seats.

"Need a ride somewhere?" she asked.

"Sure. Just home."

"Okey doke," she said.

"I love your car!" I said. It was true, even though it sounded as if I was sucking up. "When did you get it?"

"Hmmm, don't know, three months ago maybe? I've been saving, like, forever. Like since I was your age."

"Wow," I said. I didn't know how much a car cost, but I figured out that meant she'd been saving a lot for a long time. I felt embarrassed being in Jordan's cute, very clean car. I could still smell the sour grime from the arcade on me. The knees of my too big khakis were dirty from where I'd fallen.

I was quiet. She was quiet. Then suddenly, as if I'd just gotten in, Jordan turned to me and said, "Minerva Clark! How tall are you now?" She wore a fakey nice smile, where her mouth turned up but her eyes looked worried.

"I don't know." I hate it when people talk about how tall I am. Last year in sixth grade, at the end of the year, I won an award for Tallest Girl in the Class. Hannah won Friendliest Girl. Being friendly was something a person could actually *do*. Getting a prize for being tall was like getting a prize for having blood that circulated through your heart.

"And what grade are you in now? Sixth?" asked Jordan.

"Seventh."

"Wow, seventh grade."

Is this what happens to people who are about to graduate from high school? Suddenly they start acting like one of those moms who makes lame adultlike boring conversation just to have something to say? It was May, and I'd last seen Jordan at Easter, for the Annual Clark Family Million Dollar Easter Egg Hunt. (Quills hides dozens of plastic eggs around our yard with five-dollar bills inside; one egg has a twenty.) Obviously, I'd been in seventh grade then, too.

"Do you mind if we stop at Under the Covers before I drop you off? It's on the way."

"Sure. Whatever." Like I had a choice. The worst day of my life wouldn't be a true worst day unless it also involved some stupid, boring errand that seemed pointless and took about eight hundred years.

Under the Covers was a little bookstore on a wide street that had a lot of Asian restaurants, dry cleaners, nail salons, and a bead shop where my mom used to make bracelets before she and my dad got divorced a little over two years ago.

Jordan parked in front of the pizza-by-the-slice place next to the bookstore. The minute I opened the car door I got a big whiff of that hot cheese smell, my favorite food smell in all the world. I tipped my head up and sniffed.

"Smells good, don't it?" said a deep, craggy voice.

My insides jumped, although I didn't show it on the outside. A homeless guy was lazing against the low concrete wall that ran between the pizza-by-the-slice place and Under the Covers. He wore an orange bandana tied pirate-style around his head and had a white Boxer-type dog lying beside him on the sidewalk. The dog was missing one of her front legs. I tried not to stare, even though it was only a dog.

As I passed by I couldn't help myself. I reached out and gave the dog a rub on the head with my knuckles. She closed her eyes, tipped her head up. I swear she smiled a little with her rubbery black lips.

The homeless guy had been leaning back on one hand. The other hand he held in his lap, the fingers closed and bent in a way that reminded me of a wilted lily. My grandpa had had a stroke, and he had a hand like that, useless. The homeless guy straightened up suddenly and reached out and across his body. I jumped. I thought maybe he was going to grab my ankle or something, but he was just repositioning himself so he could give his dog a good scratch behind the ears. "She's a good old girl," he said. "Can't imagine life without her."

Jordan grabbed me by the upper arm and whispered, "Don't do that!"

I didn't know whether she meant pet the dog or be nice to the homeless guy. I didn't seem to ever know anything.

Inside the bookstore an old lady was standing at the counter. She had a long gray braid down her back and a tattoo of dancing fairies twirling around and up her arm. They shouldn't even let a lady with a long gray braid into a tattoo parlor. It should be like the reverse of a bar, where, if you're over twenty-one, they boot you out.

The guy behind the counter handed the lady a pen and watched while she wrote her check. When he looked up and saw Jordan and me standing there, he jumped in that way people do when someone comes up behind them and goes *Boo!*

"Jordan. How you doing?" Jordan is one of those girls no one is ever unhappy to see.

"Hey, Dwight," said Jordan.

Dwight took the lady's check, looked at it carefully, circled something on the front, and then slipped it beneath the cash drawer in the register.

"Thanks for coming in, Evelyn. I'll let you know when your order arrives," Dwight said to the lady. After she left, he straightened a stack of small books on the counter near the cash register, lining up the corners. The book was called *Bad Hair*. Dwight's hair wasn't so great itself, which made me like him. It was kind of spongy and brownish green, like something you might find growing in a forest. He wore little round glasses like Harry Potter.

"Go check out the Children's section, Minerva, why don't you?" said Jordan. "Where's the Children's section, Dwight?"

Under the Covers was so small, I could see the kids' books from where I was standing. I sighed loudly. A feeling of pure annoyance rolled over me like the chill from a sudden fear. Jordan wasn't my parent or even that day's BIC, and here she was trying to get rid of me by sending me to the kids' section.

I went over to the back wall and stared at a bunch of books I already owned. Why were Dwight and Jordan acting so nervous? Behind me I heard them whispering. For one long horrible second I thought maybe I had started my period and it was all over the back of my cargo pants. I swept my hand back there, nonchalantly, but there was nothing.

Maybe they were laughing at my Gigantor butt. I felt the campfire in my cheeks again. I was always embarrassed. Then I'd get embarrassed about being embarrassed. What was wrong with me?

I turned to look at the calender rack so my butt would face the shelves. I twirled the creaky wire rack, half full of old calendars, which mostly featured puppies. I glanced over to see Dwight hand Jordan something over the counter. She quickly tucked it into the front of her knapsack and zipped it closed.

Dwight said, "Stay out of trouble, all right?" He was half smiling. It could have been a joke, or one of those jokes that's only a joke if the other person laughs.

Jordan nodded her head once. She looked uncomfortable, like they were breaking up or something.

Suddenly, a high-pitched girl's voice said, "Hey, Jordan."

I put the basset hound calendar I was flipping through back into the wire rack and joined Jordan where she stood next to the counter. The girl with the high-pitched voice—it was almost like that of a cartoon character—was short, with kinky strawberry hair caught up in two pigtails. She wore saggy bell-bottoms that dragged on the ground, the hems crusty with mud. Where had she come from? I hadn't seen anyone enter the store.

"Did you see the story in the school paper?" the girl was saying. "I tried to get in all your great lines about how, like, our opinions should be respected even though we're still in high school. That just because we're, like, seventeen, that doesn't mean we don't know anything.

But Ms. Graham, you know the journalism teacher? She said I needed to stay on topic."

Jordan smiled—this time a real one—and collected her hair at the top of her head with one hand, then let it fall back into place. "Pansy Burrows, what are you doing here?"

Pansy Burrows drew her pale eyebrows together. "Jordan, I see you here every afternoon."

"Anyway," said Jordan, smiling her popular girl smile.

"Anyway," Pansy Burrows continued, "I said, Ms. Graham! Hel-lo! This is Jordan Parrish. She's not just anyone. She's a Rose Festival princess. I mean, ambassador. Ambassador's, like, the new word, right? Even though you still do all that kind of princessy stuff?"

Jordan was semifamous. Portland puts on the Rose Festival every June. There's the Grand Floral Parade for people who like eating blue cotton candy while watching high school marching bands play the theme song from *Gladiator*. There's also a Fun Zone down at Waterfront Park, with all those excellent rides that go upside down and backward at about ninety miles an hour.

Every high school in the city elects a Rose Festival prin—ah, *ambassador*. That's the new name. "Princess" sounds too lame and old-timey. It's always a senior girl who is smart and plays something like lacrosse and is girly but not in an obnoxious way. She is also always pretty hot. Like my cousin Jordan.

Pansy Burrows was talking nonstop about some dress that Jordan wore to the assembly where they named her Montgomery High Ambassador. I noticed sweat had popped out on the bridge of her nose. Clearly Pansy was a cling-on, high school division. I thought they only had cling-ons in middle school.

Dwight drummed the top of the cash register. Then he rearranged a collection of glittery sea-blue eyeglass cases that sat on the counter in a clear plastic tub. Some of the eyeglass cases had lemon-yellow happy faces on them, some pink peace symbols. They shone deeply, like a collection of well-polished cars.

My heart was going to stop beating out of boredom if Pansy Burrows did not stop nattering. The glittery eyeglass cases gave me an idea. I reached inside the pocket of my hoodie and gave Jupiter a nudge.

You may not know this about ferrets, but they love anything that gleams and sparkles. Jupiter could have the best time with a balled-up piece of aluminum foil. The other thing about ferrets is that they're either dead asleep or wide awake and in need of immediate entertainment.

Suddenly, his little white face poked out from the other side of my pocket and in a split second he jumped out, scooted across the counter, jumped over the stack of

Bad Hair books, and dove straight for the plastic tub of glittery eyeglass cases.

"Ack!" shrieked Pansy Burrows. "It's a rat!"

"You still got that thing?" asked Jordan, rolling her eyes.

Fast as could be Jupiter tugged the top eyeglass case out of the plastic tub and commenced to give it a good gnawing. For some reason, I noticed that this case was more purple than sea blue. Jupiter held the case between his two white paws and chewed like a little ferret maniac. But Dwight was quick. He scooped up Jupiter by his middle and looked him in the eye. "I used to have one of these guys!"

"Sorry about the case," I said. I really hadn't expected him to chew on it.

"That's okay," said Dwight. He stuck the case behind the counter. "My guy was named Toob Sock. Spelled T-O-O-B. He was black-footed, looked like a little raccoon. I miss ol' Toobie."

"I love the black-footed ones! They're so cute. I wouldn't even have a white one, except Jupiter's a dark-eyed white. I would never have, like, an albino white. They creep me out a little." I felt the campfire blaze in my cheeks. Yammer yammer yammer. I was as bad as this Pansy Burrows person.

But Dwight just nodded, as if he'd had the same

thought. "Have you seen the panda ferrets? Those are cool. Half white, half black."

"Cool," I said, making an effort to just *shut up*.

"Did you know ferret is from the old Latin? 'Fur' is thief. 'Furet' is the diminutive. It means little thief. Toobie used to steal things all the time."

He petted the top of Jupiter's head for a minute or two. I took Jupiter back and threaded him inside my pocket again. Dwight was an okay guy in my book. I bet he would like my rebuses.

Jordan and I drove up Broadway in the rain. A boy dragged a skateboard across the street in front of us and Jordan slammed on the brakes, even though it was obvious that if she'd continued driving at the same speed he would have passed safely in front of us.

"Jeez! People are insane!" She turned on the CD player. Then she turned it off. Looking back, I realize that Jordan was jittery and upset, but at the time I thought she was just irritated from having run into Cling-On Pansy Burrows.

I don't know much about driving except the basics, like stopping at a red light. You can also turn right at a red light, but only after you stop. You can't just slow down and glide around the corner, which is exactly what Jordan did at the corner of 39th and Halsey.

"Like I freaking need *this*," she said, looking in the rearview mirror. She drove old-lady slow around the corner, stopping at the curb next to a bowling alley.

Actually, she said the real F word.

I turned around to see a white police car behind us, the red and blue lights twirling on the roof. There was a long line of traffic backed up behind us. The cars slowed as they steered around us. The drivers stared at us. What if someone I knew drove by? Someone from school, or someone's mom?

I thought about ducking, but there was really nowhere to duck.

The officer got out of the patrol car, adjusted his holster, and strolled up to Jordan's window. He was so tall he needed to bend nearly in half to look in the window. He had white hair even though he didn't look very old. His eyes were pale, like the color of water in a glass.

"Do you know why I stopped you?" he asked.

"For not stopping fully at the corner?" Jordan looked up at him nervously from under her long bangs.

"Well, there's that. You also got yourself a smashed taillight. You back into a phone pole or something?"

Jordan wrinkled her nose, confused. "A smashed taillight? How?"

The officer asked for her license and registration. She

27

rummaged around in her backpack for her wallet, then reached over my bowling-ball knees to the glove box to find the registration. After she handed them over, the policeman strolled back to his white patrol car.

We sat. Jordan sniffed a little. I think she may have been crying, but I didn't dare look over.

"Quills gets pulled over a lot," I said. "The speedometer doesn't work and he never knows how fast he's going. This doesn't sound like any big deal."

"Did you notice my taillight smashed out? I just washed this two days ago."

"No," I said.

"When I picked you up, you didn't see the taillight out?"

"I don't think so," I said. There was a bad feeling cooking in my stomach. We sat there for what felt like forever. Jordan kept glancing in her side-view mirror. She then did a funny, major off-topic thing. She reached over and gave my hand a little squeeze. "Things okay at home?" she asked.

"Huh? Sure, I guess."

"Good. I'm glad." Jordan had been there the day my mom, Deedee, told her mom, my aunt Susie, that she was leaving us and moving to Santa Fe to become a yoga instructor.

Before I could say anything else, the cop returned and

instead of giving Jordan back her papers, he opened her car door. "Would you please step out, miss?"

Jordan got out without looking over at me. The officer walked behind her, leading her back to his patrol car. All I could see was his wide back, his black belt with the gun in its holster on one hip and a billy club in its holder on the other. What was going on? Where was he taking her? With a sickening jolt I realized that the worst day of my life was also probably going to be the worst day of my cousin Jordan's life.

Through the back window I watched my cousin put her hands on the roof of the car. She was wearing a long-sleeved T-shirt and low-rise jeans with a thick brown leather belt. He patted her sides, then actually pulled out a pair of real handcuffs. To tell you the truth, I thought they used these only on TV. I thought they saved them for murderers and businessmen.

Then, suddenly, there was a sharp knock at my window. For the second time in about a minute and a half I jumped.

It was another officer, the first one's partner. This policewoman wore a French braid and braces. Maybe I would be a cop when I grew up. Especially if I could wear a French braid.

"Your friend needs to come with us. Do you have someone who could come and pick you up?" She seemed pretty friendly. It was hard to remember that it was Jordan in trouble and not me. Then I remembered, I wasn't in trouble with the police, but Quills would kill me for leaving Tilt without telling anyone.

"She's not my friend, she's my cousin," I said.

"Do you have someone you can call?" the policewoman asked again.

This was a good question. I dug in my backpack for my Emergencies Only cell phone. I wanted one with red flames on the faceplate, but because it was for *emergencies only*, it was plain silver and serious. It was prepaid, with only a certain number of minutes on it. I couldn't call my dad, since he was out of town on business, like always. I couldn't call my mom, because she was divorced from my dad and living in Santa Fe, where she taught yoga.

I tried to call my oldest older brother, Mark Clark. I always call him by both names. When I was a baby I liked how they rhymed and it stuck. Plus, even though he's only twenty-four, he's really dadlike. More dadlike than my dad, actually.

The call went to voice mail. I started to get nervous. What was the point of having an Emergencies Only cell phone if in an emergency no one was around to answer it? What would they do to me if I couldn't find someone to pick me up? Would I have to go to jail, too?

Crap.

My only choice was to try flaky Morgan, my youngest older brother. I caught him between classes. He's a philosophy major at college and can't decide whether he wants to be a lawyer, like our dad, or a spoken word poet, whatever that was. At the moment, he was a junk food vegetarian, living on mostly Doritos, Mountain Dew, garden burgers, and the occasional banana, which is the junk food of the fruit kingdom.

"I need you to come get me," I squeaked into the phone. I tried to explain what had happened, that Jordan had been pulled over for rolling through a stop sign and having a smashed taillight, and now she was sitting in the back of the patrol car, waiting to be taken I didn't know where, jail or somewhere.

"They arrested her for running a stop sign?" asked Morgan. "I don't think that's legal."

"It was the stupid taillight. Or something. I don't know! I just know that someone needs to come get me! Quills is going to be so mad I left the arcade. I'm so busted!" I felt a twirl of fear in my stomach.

"They're arresting you, too? I know *that's* not legal."

"No! Not me! Jordan. They even put her in hand-cuffs."

"Min, tell me you're not making this up. Remember the Law of Karma." Morgan was also a Buddhist. I thought you had to be old to be a Buddhist, but apparently you can be a twenty-year-old college student, too. The Law of Karma, as explained to me by Morgan last year when I'd lied about eating the last piece of his birthday cake, was basically this: Every bad thing you do will one day come back and bite you in the butt; to avoid being bitten in the butt, don't do bad things.

I started to blubber for the second time that day. Morgan said, Okay, okay, he'd come get me. I told him to hang on one second, then called out the window to the police officer, who was leaning against the side of the car, examining her French braid for split ends. I guess I wasn't considered a desperate criminal in need of watching.

She asked me if Morgan would also drive the red Jetta home, or somewhere, since Jordan was our cousin. I didn't say anything, but handed the phone to the police-woman. While she and Morgan talked I reached inside my hoodie pocket to pet Jupiter. His fur was so soft.

Suddenly, from inside the car, a cell phone rang. It was *loud*. For a minute I thought it was my cell phone, but the French braid cop was still talking on it. I looked at the carpet hump between the seats and saw it was Jordan's phone.

Without thinking I answered it, just to keep it from ringing or something.

I put the phone to my ear, but before I could even say "Hey," the voice on the other end said, "I don't know why you're being such a bitch, but don't hang up on me again. You'll regret it if you do."

I snapped the phone shut fast. My knees were shaking. I turned around and looked at Jordan in the back of the police car. Her cheeks were all blotchy, as if she were crying.

I'd recognized the voice on her cell phone.

It was creepy Toc, Quills's best friend.

- 3 -

ONE OF MORGAN'S COLLEGE FRIENDS DROPPED him off at Jordan's car. Morgan talked to the French braid policewoman, signed some papers, then drove us home in Jordan's red Jetta.

"This is a pretty nice ride," said Morgan. We were stopped at a light and he tapped the gas pedal, *varooming* the engine in appreciation.

"She just got it," I said. "She's been saving up, I guess."

Morgan was wearing his favorite orange and black earflap hat, even though earflap hat weather ended months ago. In the middle of the hat he'd stuck a button that said I BLAME MY PARENTS. He switched on the radio, found a horrible jazz station. I thought my ears would bleed, it was so bad.

I bit my fingernails. I'd been doing a pretty good job lately of trying to stop. There was a thin white strip at the tip of each nail. Now, one by one, I nibbled them off. I prayed that Jordan's phone wouldn't ring again. Why was Toc calling Jordan, and why was he talking to her like that?

I thought about picking up the phone and turning it off, but then Morgan would wonder why I was fiddling with someone else's phone. Instead I prayed to the special guardian angel who watched over seventh-grade girls that the phone would stay silent, and so it did.

I couldn't stop thinking about the look on Jordan's heart-shaped face as she sat crying in the back of the patrol car. Jordan was not just a tidy girl with perfect hair and a better-than-4.0 grade-point average who looked good in hip-huggers. Sometimes the world confuses all those outside things you can see and measure with being good, but Jordan was really good. My mom and dad had the divorce sit-down with my brothers and me (we sat thigh by thigh on the sofa; Mom wept; Dad tried to make it sound as if they were only taking extremely long separate vacations) around the same time Montgomery High was beginning to cast its spring musical, which that year was *The Sound of Music*, one of those musicals I always rolled my eyes about but secretly loved.

Jordan, who was a sophomore then, had been cast as

Liesl, the oldest von Trapp daughter, who crushes on a guy named Rolfe, who is way hot but *not* a good person because he supports the Nazis. Ms. Matilda, the play's director, asked the cast members to drag in their little brothers and sisters to try out for the parts of the younger von Trapp kids. Jordan doesn't have any little sibs, and on the very afternoon my mom told my aunt Susie about the divorce—they were drinking wine out of water glasses at Aunt Susie's kitchen counter in the dead middle of the day—she dragged me down to Montgomery High to try out for the role of Louisa. I didn't want to do it, but I did it anyway, because that's how I was then, as you know.

Louisa was thirteen and moody and didn't have much to do but sing "Do Re Me" and be one of the awkward middle children. I was only eleven then, but I got the part because I could cry on cue. Blubbering all the time was what was Ms. Matilda called Louisa's "character tag," and that rainy spring blubbering was just about all I did. So, for the first time in my life, I was perfect.

Every day Jordan would pick me up from school and we would take the bus to play practice. She always brought a PayDay for each of us. We were the only people we knew who preferred PayDays to Snickers. Aunt Susie picked us up every night just as it was getting dark. Being in that play with Jordan took my mind off the fact that when I got home my mom wouldn't be there.

Jordan had been on the way to our house when she got arrested, so it was only about a ten-minute ride home, but it felt like an hour. The Electric Matador wasn't in the driveway, which meant Quills was either out looking for me and I was so dead, or else . . . there was no "or else."

We parked in front of Casa Clark, our huge old house that sticks out like a sore thumb in the neighborhood because it's a pink stucco box. All the other houses are pale gray or moss green, with shingles and wood trim. They're sweet and cottagey. Casa Clark looks like a Mexican restaurant. It has eleven bedrooms and five bathrooms and a brass fireman's pole that runs from the third floor to the kitchen. Top that.

When Morgan and I walked in, Mark Clark, my oldest older brother, was making dinner. I could hear him banging around in the kitchen, and smell his Just-Spicy-Enough Rigatoni.

I ran upstairs before Mark Clark could call me into the kitchen. I needed to IM that dog Reggie, who hadn't even missed a step after I fell off DDR and humiliated myself probably forever. Plus, Julia and the Chelseas had probably text messaged everyone and his brother by now.

Nobody was around but Hannah.

Hannahbanannah: Hey, want to go to the water park Sat.?

Ferretluver: The indoor one or the outdoor one?

Hannahbanannah: Indoor, dummy! It has all the hot guys!

Ferretluver: Sure!

Hannahbanannah: Maybe that hot guy Devon-or-Evan will be working at the snack counter. *hopes* He is sooooo hot. I know yer not into that.

Ferretluver: Into what? I'm into that.

Hannahbanannah: The last time Julia and I went to the water park, she tried to hook up with that one lifeguard dude. He's like 16! :0

Ferretluver: I'm into the water park. That red slide that goes into the deep end is so cool.

Hannahbanannah: Yah, I love that slide. We'll have to go on it lots. And hey—lucky there's not DDR at the water park. *poke*

Ferretluver: ??

Hannahbanannah: Chelsea de G said it was like t-i-m-b-e-r! She can be so mean.

While Hannah and I had been IMing I'd opened the top drawer of my desk and pulled out my rebus notebook. Hannah didn't know I kept a rebus notebook. I read my last one:

FUSS
nothing

Big fuss over nothing.

I felt a sadness whoosh up inside of me, like the tide coming in. Making rebuses used to make me happier than just about anything.

I could not possibly go to the water park. I said, "sure," a version of "yes," but of course I meant "no." I would die before I went to the water park. The only bathing suit I owned was from last summer, when my mom showed up for a few weeks and bought me a red Speedo with yellow flowers that was an extra long. I complained I didn't *need* an extra long. My mom said I would grow into it. I was five-eight already. How much more growing did she expect me to do? She said she wished I wouldn't back talk. I wasn't back talking. I was making a point. The bathing suit had one of those horrible ladyish built-in shelf-bra things. I wore a T-shirt over it. It hid everything except of course my Gigantor thighs and bowling-ball knees.

"MIN-ER-VA!" It was Mark Clark, hollering up the stairs at me.

In the kitchen, my brother stood at the stove in his businessman-casual khaki pants and polo shirt, stirring the sauce for his Just-Spicy-Enough Rigatoni in a big aluminum pot, humming along to some band from the eighties playing on the kitchen boom box.

I loved my brother pretty much more than anyone, but even I had to admit that he was really a geek. And I don't mean computer geek, even though he was that, too. He worked at a big corporation making sure no one could hack into their computer system, which is pretty ironic, since when he was about my age he was a computer hacker.

Morgan was sitting on the counter drinking a Mike's Hard Lemonade.

"You're not old enough to be drinking that," I said.

"Tell Mark what happened with Jordan," said Morgan, taking a huge swallow.

"So she ran a stop sign and they hauled her off to jail? That doesn't sound right. Had she been drinking?" said Mark Clark.

"No. I don't know. I don't think so." I got a diet cream soda from the fridge.

"Maybe she had some speeding tickets and there was a bench warrant out for her arrest," said Morgan. "They can do that if you don't pay your tickets. Very uncool from a karmic perspective, but it does happen."

Morgan and his dumb karma. I rolled my eyes.

"Still, it doesn't sound right. Jordan's always been so squared away," said Mark Clark.

I pulled up a stool at the kitchen counter. Mark Clark wanted me to tell the whole story from the beginning. I thought, *Why do you even care?*

Then we heard the back door open and slam shut. "Is she here?" Uh-oh. Quills.

I was relieved to see that creepy Toc wasn't with him. Quills's face was totally blank. That's how you knew you were in big trouble with Quills. Except when occasionally he had a hissy fit. Then, look out.

He opened a cupboard, got out a glass, and set it on the counter. With his back still to us he said, "What in the HELL happened to you? You don't just leave without telling someone."

"I tried to call."

"I spent about twelve hours looking around that stupid mall."

"It's only five o'clock. We didn't get to Tilt until one o'clock. You could have only spent four hours," I said. "Didn't Reggie tell you? Reggie should have told you."

"According to Reggie, you left without telling him, either."

I took a swig of my diet cream soda. It was extra fizzy and tickled my nose. Outside, the rain spattered against the windows. Left without telling Reggie! Like Reggie is my parent? Reggie was my best friend and should have come after me when I ran out of the arcade, and here I was getting yelled at. The tears wobbled in my eyes. Would this worst day ever ever *ever* NEVER end?

No one said anything.

This was the advantage of living with boys. If my mom was still around, she'd yell at me. She'd ask me what I was thinking, or why I wasn't thinking, and did I know I'd worried her half to death. I probably should have said "Sorry" to Quills, but I didn't feel like it. Maybe Reggie wasn't such a dog. Maybe he didn't tell Quills I fell off DDR and made a humongous fool out of myself. My back was starting to hurt from my bad landing.

I walked to the dry-erase board and wrote:

Arrest
You're

"You're under arrest. That's my special Jordan rebus."

"Whaz up with that?" said Quills.

"Jordan was giving me a ride home from Tilt and she was pulled over and hauled off downtown to jail," I said, giving him the *TV Guide* version of events. I didn't want to think about it or talk about it.

"You mean like in handcuffs?" said Quills. "Cool."

"No, *not* cool!" I shrieked. My nerves were shot.

"We'll talk about it later," said Mark Clark. "But let me finish my point. Min, if you *ever*, and I mean *ever*,

42

get pulled over, or anything like that ever happens to you—"

"Don't say anything until you talk to a lawyer," Morgan interrupted. I don't think Morgan liked it when Mark Clark talked all lawyery like our dad. Morgan was the would-be-lawyer-in-training. Mark Clark was already the oldest and a computer genius. Wasn't that enough?

"Not the Lecture!" Since our dad was a lawyer, I'd been hearing this speech since before I could walk. I was so relieved not to be in more trouble, I thought it was safe to get a little snotty. I took a big gulp of soda, then burped.

"Hey, good one," said Morgan. He took a drink of Mike's and tried one, but it was wussy in comparison.

Quills said, "You are both pathetic—" and then he burped *losers*, really loud. *Looooooo-sseerrrrs!* We all howled. It was an all-is-forgiven moment.

"Let me finish my point here," said Mark Clark. "If you ever get pulled over, don't say anything until you talk to a lawyer."

"You have the right to remain silent," said Morgan.

"I don't really expect you to put yourself in a situation where the cops would have any reason to detain you—"

"Mark! I got it! Gawd!" I wish I could say that only your mom or dad have the ability to make you roll your eyes, but it can happen with your lecturey older brother, too.

Suddenly, the phone rang. With all the cell phones in the house, almost no one ever called on the real phone, which hung on the kitchen wall. Morgan answered it; we heard a funny click and traded glances. Morgan pressed a button and put us on speaker phone.

We made our voices go all high. In unison we said, "Hi, Charlie!"

Our dad's name was actually Howard, but because we never really saw him, and when we talked to him it was always on speaker phone, we called him Charlie, the invisible boss from *Charlie's Angels*.

"I just called to see how your art opening went, Mark," said Dad. He was at that moment in New York on business.

"It's tonight," said Mark Clark. "Starts at seven."

"I knew that!" said Dad, which he obviously didn't.

For a few minutes Mark Clark and Dad talked about Mark's new exhibit, which I, like my dad, had forgotten about completely. Since it had nothing to do with me— or not at that very moment, anyway—I spaced out. I thought about what my hair must have looked like when I fell off DDR. It had been in a ponytail, but the scrunchie had come out. I must have looked monster scary.

Then I heard Mark Clark say, "I bet I can get Minerva to give me a hand."

"Sure," I said automatically. I thought maybe he was talking about pouring the rigatoni into the strainer, or making garlic bread, or something.

"It won't take long," said Mark Clark.

"Whatever." I wondered if maybe the scrunchie was still on the floor of the arcade. Someone had probably taken it, or maybe the janitor picked it up. Would a scrunchie be something the janitor would take to the lost and found, or would he toss it out? I was pretty sure that he would toss out a plain elastic ponytail holder, because it looked so much like a rubber band. This is what I was thinking about when I said yes to the thing that would change my life.

"Don't say okay until you know what you're agreeing to," said Charlie over the speaker phone.

But it was too late. I'd already said okay. That was the bad part about living with all boys. Once you said you'd do something, you were expected to do it.

- 4 -

SEVEN THIRTY P.M. WORST DAY IN the Life of
Minerva Suzanne Clark. Trapped in the backseat of the
Electric Matador.

"I'm not sitting in front of a bunch of people with
electrodes connected to my head," I said.

Mark Clark, Quills, and I were driving downtown to
the Narino Art Gallery, where Mark Clark was having an
art show of his fractals.

"You already said yes," said Mark Clark. "I need you
to help me out. And once they see the fractal I'll make
from your brain waves, everyone will want one. You'll be
the most popular kid at the gallery."

"I'll be the only kid at the gallery."

"That should make you feel better, then. No one

to see Mark Clark make a fool out of ya," said Quills.

"I don't want to do it. You shouldn't make me do something I don't want to do. It's bad parenting."

Quills and Mark Clark roared with laughter. Quills spit out the SweetTart he was sucking on. I then heard about eight hundred hours' worth of stories about how it was when they were growing up with Mom and Dad living together in Casa Clark, and how they had to clean the garage every Saturday and take showers every night and blah blah blah.

We parked two blocks away from the Narino Gallery, in front of a big warehouse that now housed a fancy sushi place and an antiques store. The air was warm and sticky. I snuck a whiff of my pits; I'd forgotten to put on deodorant after my shower. How could I have forgotten? How could I be so dang stupid all the time?

This was so totally unfair. Inequitable is what it was. Maybe I'd be a Gigantor my whole life, a snarly-headed loser who said yes to stuff without thinking, but I would have a good vocabulary.

Have you ever noticed that all art galleries look just like art galleries do in the movies? It's always wood floors and white walls with a row of pictures all in a line, and not too close. Mark Clark's fractals were big

47

and bright. They looked like hippie posters dripping with color, or pictures of the human body as seen through an electron microscope, or those bright snow-flakes at the end of a kaleidoscope. Sometimes they looked like pictures of complicated shorelines as seen from outer space.

I made a beeline past the fractals to the table at the back of the gallery, where there were all kinds of weird-looking grown-up snacks. I grabbed a handful of pale yellow crackers and stuffed them in my sweatshirt pocket. Then I remembered that Jupiter had taken a long nap in my pocket only hours before. Was it still gross to eat the crackers if no one but me knew Jupiter had been in there?

Mark Clark stood in the middle of a circle of grown-ups with sleek shoes and good manners. They held glasses of wine that they didn't drink. The ladies all had big rings on their bony fingers. They looked young, but you could tell they weren't. They had very neat hair. I thought they were rich people, and not the computer nerds Mark Clark worked with. Otherwise, they'd know about fractals, wouldn't they?

". . . all computer generated," Mark Clark was saying as I stood next to him. He propped his elbow on my shoulder, as if it were a ledge. "These are basically prints of electronic images derived from mathematical equations.

They're so hypnotic because there's only one shape in the fractal, and it's repeated over and over and over again, to infinity."

The people around him with the wineglasses nodded.

"A very simple example would be a fractal composed of small squares that creates, let's say, a large propeller shape. If you zoom in on the propeller, you'll see the smaller squares. The computer uses basic geometric shapes to create complex shapes, but if you looked closely at the simple shapes, you'd see the complex shapes inside of them."

"But how do they know how to form themselves into a propeller?" asked a woman with her blond hair twisted up in a bun.

"That's where the math comes in," said Mark Clark, rubbing his hands together and grinning in a dorky imitation of a movie villain. "Every equation begins with a seed number. You'll see. At eight o'clock, I'm going to demonstrate how it works."

The people with the shoes and the wineglasses started talking about the rise of computers in modern life and then, like always, one of them asked Mark Clark a question about why her printer didn't work.

I wandered around and snuck a cracker now and then from my pocket. I had seen all these fractals before. There was "I Am a Rock," where the seed number was extracted from something having to do with the way light hit a piece of gray stone in our side yard, and "Groove Is in the Heart," made from Jupiter's heartbeat.

Through the big glass front door I saw Quills pacing up and down, talking on his cell phone. He was mad about something and almost crashed into one couple hurrying through the door. I wondered if he was talking to that creepy Toc.

Morgan showed up with some girl with a head of very cool blond dreadlocks. Since they were college students, they made a point of standing in front of each fractal and impressing themselves and each other with a lot of big words. I heard the dreadlocks girl say "fantasia of color." What did that even mean? I thought only boys could be poseurs. Note to self: Ask Reggie. Could girls be poseurs, too?

As the gallery filled up I started getting stomachache nervous. It was almost eight o'clock. The food table had been moved against one wall and another table was being set up by a few computer nerds Mark Clark knew from work. I recognized them because sometimes they came over with their six-packs of beer and family-size bags of M&M's to play video games. They put equipment on the table: a machine Mark Clark had made himself from parts he got at Radio Shack, a laptop, some kind of a printer, and other stuff.

I said "Hey" to DeMaio, who was Mark Clark's assistant at work. DeMaio had a first name, but no one ever used it. He was just DeMaio. He was the tallest person I knew, and he had kinky black hair that he wore in a ponytail. It was so kinky the ponytail looked like a pinecone.

DeMaio was the one who got Mark Clark into fractals. Mark Clark said DeMaio was a fractal freak, and I knew he was here tonight to deliver his Fractal Manifesto. Mark Clark is just that kind of geek: He knows people who have manifestos.

"Everyone! Gather round!" yelled DeMaio to the people in the gallery. He was wearing a black velvet cloak, which made me think of magicians. DeMaio gestured with his long arms all dramatically. "Come see a fractal in the making!"

Mark Clark stood with his back to the gathering crowd. He booted up his laptop, turned on his machine, which was about the size of a microwave, but with various colored switches and dials, and plugged in a bunch of thin gray wires.

I felt my hands start to sweat.

I felt my feet start to sweat.

"Sit down, Min," he said. I sat in a white wooden chair next to the table. I started bouncing my leg, all nervous. Why why WHY had I said I'd do this?

This reminded me of one of my all-time best rebuses:

D
UC
K

Sitting duck. That was me.

From where I sat I could see straight through the middle of the gallery and out the front door. Quills was still on his cell phone. The sky behind him was the same color as a bruise I once got on my thigh when I fell off my skateboard. Suddenly, there was a crack of thunder, like giants were bowling. More thunder. Quills turned up the collar of his army jacket; it whipped against his cheek in the wind.

Mark Clark took the spongy ends of the electrodes and dipped them in a bowl of salt water. He told the crowd salt water conducts electricity best.

He then put one electrode on each temple, one behind my ear, and one smack in the middle of my forehead. Suddenly, I wasn't just nervous, but a little pissed off. Mark Clark was making me look stupid, with this electrode in the middle of my forehead, like I was some doofus in a lab experiment.

All this time, DeMaio was giving his manifesto. You could tell he loved having an audience. "What one must appreciate is not simply the beauty of the fractals, but also their *perfection*."

Mark Clark fiddled with his machines. As if from far away, I heard him tell DeMaio to tell his audience that he was now recording my brain waves on his laptop. Everyone was staring at me like I was some freak show freak. I *was* a freak show freak. Why else would my parents have basically left me to be raised by my brothers, who turned me into a lab rat for art?

"Even the brain waves of a thirteen-year-old girl can produce a gloriously perfect work of art," DeMaio was saying. "Perfect and beautiful. Total perfection."

The audience smirked—I knew that look!—and a clap of thunder hit us, as if a giant had dropped a bowling ball right onto the roof.

DeMaio jumped, startled. He was saying, "beauty of perfection."

Then it was like a black curtain came down in front of a stage, only the curtain was smack in front of my eyeballs. That's the last thing I remember: the word "perfection" and that window-rattling thunder, before everything went black.

- 5 -

WHEN i OPENED MY EYES i thought I was in my room. But the bed wasn't my bed. It was too high. The light in the room was low and the air smelled funny, sour but clean. The bed was surrounded by white curtains. Then Mark Clark's face was in front of mine. He bent over me. He said, "Thank God."

Quills stood at his shoulder, tugging at his short crayon-yellow blond hair. "Jeez, Min, you scared the living sh—snot out of us."

Morgan stood up from where he sat in a chair on the other side of my bed. He'd taken off his earflap hat. Unlike the rest of us Clarks who had thick reddish brown hair, Morgan had a mess of wispy dirty-blond curls that were plastered against the sides of his head, giving him a

54

mean case of hat hair. "I'll get the doc," he said, slipping through the curtains.

Was I in the hospital? For some reason, my teeth hurt, as if I had just had my braces tightened and gotten new elastics.

Mark Clark took my hand. He looked . . . Could he have been *crying*?

"Why am I here?" I asked. Someone had taken off my shoes and socks. For some reason, I kept thinking, "Perfection."

Perfection?

Mark Clark must have known I was all right, because he clicked into semilecture mode and started giving me some long sciencey explanation about how the Narino Gallery was in a one-hundred-year-old brick building and had one-hundred-year-old electrical outlets. The building was struck by lightning and there was a power surge, which is when too much electrical power is forced through the lines, and then somehow, because I was hooked up to Mark Clark's fractal-making laptop, the electricity surged into me. It didn't help that I was wearing my purple Chuck Taylor high tops, with their thin soles, which allowed the electricity to zap right on up to the top of my brain. Or something like that.

Then Mark Clark said that he had tracked down our parents, or tried to. Charlie was tied up with some big lawyery business deal in New York City, but would call the next day to see how I was, and if he needed to cancel the conference or the summit or whatever it was, he would cancel it and come straight home. Deedee was in some mountains somewhere on a yoga retreat and couldn't be reached at all.

Dr. Wong came through the curtains, with Morgan right behind him. He had very warm hands and short spiky black hair. He looked more like a snowboarder than a doctor. He asked whether any part of me was numb or tingling. He looked inside my mouth and asked me to say, "Peter Piper picked a peck of pickled peppers."

"Was I electrocuted?" I asked.

Quills laughed a little and Mark Clark gave him a look. "If you were electrocuted you wouldn't be here, Minnie Mouse." I hated when Quills called me that.

"Where would I be?" I asked.

"Pushing up the daisies! Singing with the choir invisible," said Quills. I knew that meant dead.

"It was an electric shock," said Dr. Wong. "You're going to be all right. Not to worry."

Then Mark Clark and Dr. Wong started doing that adult thing where they talk over your head, as if you're not there. They talked about what medical tests I should take to make sure I was okay.

Dr. Wong asked me some more questions about how I

felt. Mostly, I felt peaceful and weirdly empty of the normal thoughts that filled up my head all the time. When the lightning hit the building, I had jerked up out of my chair and slammed onto the floor, as if I were getting knocked around by an angry ghost. I must have looked like I was spazzing big-time, way worse than when I fell off DDR at Tilt.

Then Morgan got that funny frown that I knew meant his cell phone was vibrating in his pocket. He flipped it open. "This is Morgan . . . I'm not sure tonight is good . . . It's already, what, nine thirty . . . I think one of us will be around tomorrow . . ." He covered the speaker part of the phone with his thumb.

"Jordan just got sprung. She wants to come and get her car."

"I guess she isn't the hardened criminal we all thought," said Quills.

"What did she *do*?" I asked. I'd forgotten all about poor Jordan getting hauled off to jail. Had that really happened today?

"Tell her she can come tomorrow morning," said Mark Clark.

I guess I'd have to wait to find out.

The next day I didn't have to go to school, in case I suddenly keeled over from having been electrocuted and all. Plus, Mark Clark was going to be the BIC and take me to some special doctor. Plus Charlie was probably going to show up and act all concerned.

When I woke up I went right to my desk and took out my rebus journal. I wrote:

FREE + 🔑

Freaky.

It was kind of lame, but I didn't care. I liked making up rebuses, and that was all that counted. I still had that strange peaceful feeling, which got a little stranger.

I looked over and caught a glimpse of myself in the long mirror hanging on the back of my door. The edges of the mirror were covered with glittery stars and snowflakes and happy faces stuck there so I wouldn't have to look at myself.

The girl I saw today was tall. She wore a pair of blue flannel pj bottoms with cowboy boots and hats on them and a black Humongous Bag of Cashews T-shirt with a giant cashew on the front that unfortunately looked more like a banana. Her face was square and she had a nice straight nose. She had curly/wavy/straight hair that was an unusual reddish brown.

I stood up and went straight to the mirror. I looked at my long arms and long feet. I always thought I was a fat

Gigantor freak show freak, but I wasn't. I wasn't fat at all. I wasn't skinny, but I wasn't fat. I was okay.

I checked around inside my head to see if I could find my usual feelings when I looked at myself, the feeling like I wanted to hide under my bed forever. But there was nothing wrong with me, nothing that I could see. My mind felt swept clean of all my usual feelings of self-hatred. Without them, I had nothing to think about. What was with that?

Downstairs, I heard people talking, Mark Clark and someone else.

I snuck downstairs. At the bottom of the stairs I looked across the hallway to the computer room, where Mark Clark has two computers set up against the big windows. Outside, fat pink rhododendrons pressed against the glass.

Mark Clark stood by his desk, his hand on the back of the chair. Behind him I saw a video game on his computer screen. Probably EverQuest. Playing EQ was what Mark Clark did instead of go out on dates. He had that interrupted look he always gets when anyone tries to talk to him when he's on EQ.

Jordan and her best friend, Tiffani Hollingsworth, stood in the middle of the room with their backs to the door. Jordan and Tiffani had been best friends since kindergarten. Tiffani was just as pretty as Jordan, but where Jordan was tall and fair, Tiffani was short and dark. Her real hair color was semisweet chocolate brown like Liv Tyler from *The Lord of the Rings*, but she dyed it light brown like Jordan's, and ironed it straight like hers, too.

They both wore low-rise cords with thick black belts. Tiffani's trademark accessories were platform sandals, the kind with the heavy wooden soles that weighed about ten tons. The kind that, when they slide off your feet, you sometimes come down on the edge of the platform with the bare underside of your foot and it feels as if you're going to be crippled for life.

I know because I used to wear them around when Tiffani would babysit me two years ago, when everyone still thought I needed a babysitter. Reggie stopped having a babysitter when he was, like, in third grade.

". . . and then, after they got me down to the police station and took my fingerprints, they realized it wasn't even me!" said Jordan. "The person they originally arrested back on Valentine's Day had given the cops my information, but our fingerprints didn't match. So they let me go, and I called Tiffani to come and get me!" Jordan was talking faster than I'd ever heard her talk before, plucking up her hair and letting it fall over her shoulders again and again. I noticed that she was wearing a necklace I'd never seen before, a small gold J filled with tiny diamonds. Those couldn't be real diamonds, could they? My aunt Susie was a single mom with about ten jobs, and Jordan had had to save up for her car.

"Someone got arrested for something else and gave them Jordan's name," added Tiffani. "Then, when she didn't show up in court for her hearing, a warrant was put out for the real Jordan's arrest. Or something. I think that's how it works." She giggled even though it wasn't funny.

"That's how it works," said Mark Clark. "It's called identity theft."

"Is that a new shirt, Mark? The color's really good on you. It brings out the blue in your eyes," said Tiffani.

Was Tiffani hitting on my brother? Eeeeow.

"But didn't they take a mug shot of the original person when they arrested him, er, her?" I asked. It just leaped out of my mouth.

Both Jordan and Tiffani spun around, surprised. They looked me up and down. I was still wearing my pj's, and my hair was snarling up pretty good on one side.

"How you doing?" Mark Clark asked, all concerned. I could tell he still felt pretty guilty about my getting electrocuted.

"Like . . . like . . . gack . . ." I stuck my tongue out and put my hands around my throat, like I was choking myself.

"Hey, people die from electric shocks every day," he said.

"Not in an art gallery getting a fractal made from their brain waves in front of a bunch of strangers," I said. I was surprised at my tone—normally I'm not allowed to give tone—but I felt entitled, somehow.

Jordan wanted to know what happened and I filled her in, even though I really didn't want to talk about it.

"Well, cousin, just don't let anyone ever say you don't look beautiful in the morning," said Jordan, punching my shoulder.

"I won't," I said, punching her right back.

I could tell she was only half teasing, but for some reason I didn't really care. Weird, huh? Before I got electrocuted I might have *said*, "I won't," but it would be just to look like I didn't care, but inside I *would* care. Inside, I would worry about what Jordan really meant and how Gigantor ugly she thought I really looked. But I knew that besides my messy hair I just looked like my normal Minerva self.

Jordan and Tiffani traded one of those "what's up with her?" glances.

I was more interested in Jordan's identity theft. I knew from TV they always took mug shots.

"That's the totally sucky part," said Tiffani, adjusting her rubber bracelets. "They had a mug shot of the original person, but it was around the same time the police department switched to digital cameras—"

"I read about that in the paper," said Mark Clark. "They lost about ten days' worth of photos because they forgot to upload pictures onto the hard drive."

"So they lost the picture of the person who said she was me," said Jordan. "It's lucky our fingerprints weren't close. They're even wondering whether maybe a guy didn't do it since Jordan is both a boy's name and a girl's name . . ." Jordan shrugged. You could tell she was just glad it was over.

"I still just can't believe they didn't think to upload the mug shots. It's so nice to know the safety of the entire city rests in the hands of people who forgot they actually need to save the pictures they were taking *onto* something. Everyone! Off my planet!" Mark Clark made a gesture as if to banish the world's meatheads.

Jordan and Tiffani giggled down into their hands so that their hair swung forward on either side of their heads, perfect shiny curtains of perfect straight hair. For some strange reason, I didn't envy their hair anymore. In place of my thoughts about how my life would be one hundred percent better if I had perfect shiny swinging hair was something else, something more interesting.

"So what do you do about the identity theft?" I asked.

"I don't think it's any big deal now that the cops have

it all straightened out," said Jordan. "I doubt it'll happen again."

"But it happened *this* time. Don't you *care* that someone went to all that trouble to give them your name? I mean, why your name? Why didn't they just give them some random fake name?"

"Could I get my keys now?" Jordan asked Mark Clark, turning away from me. It seemed as if she was ignoring me, but I couldn't be sure.

"I really like your necklace," I said to her back. "Are those real diamonds?"

"Thanks," she said, but she wouldn't look at me.

- 6 -

CHARLIE CALLED TO CHECK UP on me, and when it was clear that I wasn't going to be a vegetable for the rest of my life, he went about his lawyery business, promising to be home very soon. In Charlie's world "very soon" meant whenever you see the whites of my eyes. Mark Clark took me to the doctor, just like he always took me everywhere. Quills came along for moral support, whatever that was. The doctor was a special kids' brain doctor, recommended by Dr. Wong. We drove in Mark Clark's car, an old BMW that used to belong to Charlie. It was gray and Dadlike, just like Mark Clark.

The brain doctor's office was near the Rose Garden, where our basketball team, the Portland Trail Blazers, play all their home games, and where famous bands have their concerts.

"Hey, Metallica's coming to town," said Quills from the backseat. "They rule."

I shrugged. "Aren't they, like, eight hundred years old?"

"Dude, it's like going to the Louvre to see the Mona Lisa or one of those really old paintings," said Quills. "For the true musician it's research."

"Then why are *you* going? Ha ha ha."

Quills reached over the backseat and pulled my hood.

"Hey there," said Mark Clark.

"Yeah, I've got fried brains, didn't you hear? I'm a delicate flower."

"You're a smart-aleck, is what you are. I would have never been able to get away with the back talk you do," said Quills.

"Maybe that's because my back talk's better than yours was, more *entertaining*."

Quills snorted. Mark Clark just laughed. I was a little shocked at what was coming out of my mouth myself. I put my feet up on the dashboard and retied my purple Chuck Taylors.

One of the lanes was closed for construction. Then one of those giant yellow hole diggers that boys always think are so awesome backed into our lane, blocking it completely. The light turned green, but we weren't going anywhere.

It turned out we were stuck near Under the Covers, the same bookstore I'd gone to with Jordan the day before. Was it really yesterday? I felt like a different person somehow.

There was yellow police tape strung across the glass front door. It said POLICE LINE DO NOT CROSS. Inside, you could see the wire postcard racks and a bunch of big cops standing around with their hands on their hips.

"I wonder what's going on over there," I said.

"Cool—a robbery," said Quills.

"Or something worse," said Mark Clark. "They usually don't waste the tape for a simple robbery."

My oldest older brother was right; it was something worse. Way worse. I don't know how I knew this, I just did. And suddenly I also knew I had to check it out for myself.

Before I even knew I was doing it, I took Jupiter out of where he was snoozing in my hoodie pocket and plopped him in Mark Clark's lap. Some Minerva Clark I did not recognize threw open the door and jumped out of the car, slid between two parked cars at the curb, and ducked right under the police tape, just like it was the most normal thing. I heard the muffled sound of Mark Clark and Quills squawking from inside the car.

Inside Under the Covers some of the policemen were just standing around, conversations coming out of the walkie talkies stuck in their belts. One of them was wearing really strong aftershave. They didn't notice me.

Behind the counter, a guy in a sports coat the color and texture of a granola bar was leaning over Jordan's friend Dwight, the one who'd owned Toob Sock, the black-footed ferret. I peeked around the counter and saw Dwight lying on the floor on his back, rolled half on one hip, as if he'd fallen. I could see only his head poking out from behind where he'd undoubtedly fallen. His head was tilted slightly away from me, as if he were gazing up at the shelves filled with books that lined the back wall of the store.

I stood there and stared, like I had every right to be there. Poor Dwight's Harry Potter glasses were missing, and there was a meaty gash on the left side of his head, deep red blood darker than it ever is on *Law & Order*, shining around the wound, matted in his hair. Dwight's eyes were closed, but his mouth was opened just a little. You could see the bottom of his chipped front tooth. I kept thinking, *Why is Dwight lying behind the counter taking a nap?* Weird, huh? Obviously he wasn't sleeping.

He was dead.

I was looking at a dead person.

I had to look away. I had to look at something else. I

stared at the cover of *Bad Hair*. It had a photograph of a boy with thick wavy red hair wearing an orange turtleneck. Then the plastic bucket of glittery sea-blue eyeglass cases caught my eye. I looked a little closer. The more-purple-than-blue one that Jupiter had gnawed on wasn't there. Who would buy an eyeglass case with teeth marks on one end? Or maybe Dwight had just gotten rid of it. I thought about how Dwight hadn't gotten mad, even though Jupiter had wrecked his merchandise. He was amused. He was a nice guy, a good person, and here he was dead on the floor of this quiet bookstore.

Too Much Aftershave yelled, "Hey! What's she doing here!" He was about ten feet tall and had an army haircut, where you could see his skull through the haircut. His scalp glistened with sweat. His red face was crumpled in irritation or anger or both. I stood there and looked right at him. I hadn't cringed when he hollered. I didn't cry, or worry that he was thinking, *Who* is *this double freak show freak?* I wasn't worried at all.

"Miss, this is a crime scene. You can't be here." A Latino cop with the whitest teeth ever took me by my upper arm.

"I got a phone call about a book," I lied. "And I'm here to pick it up."

"You can get it another time," said White Teeth.

"But I need it for a report," I said. "It's due tomorrow." I smiled and shrugged.

"From who?" asked Too Much Aftershave.

"Who what?" I said.

"Who called you? And when?"

"I don't know," I said. "Someone called saying my book was here. They left the message on my voice mail."

"It wasn't him, was it?" Too Much Aftershave pointed at Dwight.

"Oh no! It was a girl. A lady." Along the wall behind the counter was a floor-to-ceiling bookcase. On one shelf there was a row of books with squares of paper held to the spines with rubber bands. On each square there was a name. I guessed these were books on hold.

"That's mine right there," I pointed in the direction of the books. I had about three seconds to figure out which title looked like something I would order.

"*Bridal Bargains: Secrets to Throwing a Fantastic Wedding on a Realistic Budget*. You getting married or something?" said Too Much Aftershave.

"No, that one over there." I pointed to the far end of the case.

He leaned over to read the spine. "*Professional Real Estate Development?*"

"Yeah, that's it," I said. "It's for a report."

"So you said," said Too Much Aftershave. He had

pale psycho killer eyes. He turned and glared as he took the piece of paper from around the book. He read the name on the paper.

"What's your report about, Miss . . . Takimoto?"

"Get her out of here," said one of the other cops. "We've got the medical examiner on his way."

I took the book, turned, and walked out of Under the Covers very fast, the way they tell you to walk when there's a fire drill at school. Too Much Aftershave didn't ask if I wanted to pay for the book. As I slipped between the two cars still parked at the curb, I started shaking. Part of it was seeing Dwight dead, but part of it was also that I didn't recognize myself. Who was that girl who acted as if she had every right to be there, who wanted to hang around as long as possible just to . . . just to . . . I didn't know what . . . just to look? It was as if I'd had an out-of-body experience without ever leaving my body.

The BMW was just where I'd left it, stuck behind the yellow hole digger. As I opened the door, Mark Clark shouted, "What was *that*?"

When Mark Clark got mad, the sparkle went out of his big blue eyes. We called it his Paid Assassin Look, and he was throwing his Paid Assassin Look my way as he dumped poor Jupiter back in my lap.

"You're hurting my ferret," I said. "Be gentle."

"You don't just jump out of the car in traffic! What's wrong with you?" said Mark Clark.

"There happens to be a dead person in there. Jordan's friend Dwight, the bookstore guy."

I could see by the looks on my brothers' faces that they were worried, but I hadn't done anything dangerous. What I'd done was just a non-Minerva-type thing to do. I felt my heart beating in my neck. Now I was irritated. "And I didn't jump out of the car in traffic. We're just sitting here."

"Dead? Like, murdered?" asked Quills. "Cool."

"It was not cool!" I shouted. "It was awful."

"Take it easy," said Mark Clark. The warmth returned to his eyes. He patted my knee. "What's going on with you?"

What *was* going on with me?

That's what we'd come to Dr. Lozano to find out. Dr. Lozano had a tiny gold nose ring and was as short as the shortest girl in my class. She wore blue slacks and a handwoven vest with crocodiles on it. She shook each of our hands, and hers were so thin and small, I looked down to make sure she wasn't short a few fingers. I picked her hand up before she snatched it away and said, "You have the smallest hands on a grown-up I think I've ever seen."

There was a weird moment when no one said anything, though I could practically feel the words "Don't be rude, Minerva" forming themselves in Mark Clark's big computer genius brain. But then Dr. Lozano laughed, clapped her narrow hands together, and said, "That I do. That I do."

Have you ever been aware of the moment you have a thought for the very first time in your entire life? At that moment I had this thought: Being a grown-up and being less than five feet tall might be worse than being a five-eight thirteen-year-old. People might not take you very seriously. They might think you look like a doll.

Dr. Lozano led me back into her office, where she showed me some paint splotches and asked me what I thought they were, then asked me to fill in a peg board with yellow pegs. She tested my hand-eye coordination and gave me a questionnaire with about eight hundred questions on it.

She asked me to draw a self-portrait.

I felt myself getting impatient. This was stupid. I was totally fine. All I could think of was seeing Dwight—I mean Dwight's body—lying there on the floor. I could only think of his mouth open that little bit and how he'd been so nice to me that day in the bookstore. Who could have wanted him dead? He didn't seem like the kind of person to have any enemies. And had Jordan heard the news yet? They were pretty good friends. My mind was doing a push-me pull-you thing, where it wanted to go in two different directions at the same time.

Finally, Dr. Lozano brought in Mark Clark. He must have told Dr. Lozano over the phone that our dad was on a business trip and our mom lived in Santa Fe, because she talked to him just as if he were my parent, which, of course, he pretty much was.

She asked him about my habits, what I ate, how much I back talked. Since the accident, had he noticed anything different about the way I acted? Had I slept all right the night before? Did I repeat myself when I talked? Did I look in the mirror a lot?

Mark Clark pulled on his goatee, pondering. "She's more . . . inquisitive?" He told her how I jumped out of the car and ran into Under the Covers and how unlike me that was. "Bolder," he said.

"Hmmmm," said Dr. Lozano. She entered this information into her computer.

"This is very interesting," she said finally. "I've seen this only once before, with Caleb Presinger, a boy a little older than Minerva who was shocked while trying to build an electric chair for a haunted house." Mark Clark must have made a face, because then she said, "Not a *real* electric chair. It delivered a low-voltage shock. Nothing serious."

"Unless you were Caleb Presinger," I said.

Dr. Lozano laughed. "Yes, I suppose you're right."

"Minerva's cognitive skills are fine, and so are her motor skills. All good news. However, she did score moderately low on the TSSA—the Test of Serious Symptoms of Adolescence—and significantly low on the TPS, which is a major indicator of what we're looking at here."

"TPS? Isn't that like a television station?" I said. I knew it wasn't. It sounded funny, though.

"The Think Poorly of Self test. I've yet to meet a girl in Minerva's age range who scores lower than a fifty. Minerva scored a two."

"Meaning what?" asked Mark Clark.

"I'm not sure exactly," said Dr. Lozano. "I don't think the full effects of her shock are known yet, but from the looks of things, I'd say that Minerva has suffered a loss of the self-consciousness that's so typical in girls her age. Somehow, the shock rewired her sense of self. According to these test results, she now thinks she's perfect just the way she is."

Mark Clark looked over at me. I gave him my bug-eyed look.

"But how will that manifest itself? How will she be different?"

"Who knows?" said Dr. Lozano. "We so rarely see

75

girls this age who aren't utterly consumed with how they look or don't look. It's hard to say what will happen."

What I got out of what Dr. Lozano was saying was that I used to think I was a freak show freak but not anymore.

That doesn't sound like such a big deal, does it? But it was.

- 7 -

MARK CLARK HAS AN OBNOXIOUS HABIT of assigning chores the minute you walk in the door. I was sure he would still do this to me even though I was now, according to Dr. Lozano, officially impaired.

When we got home, I ran to my room up on the third floor and cranked up Green Day. I always make sure the music is not so loud that I get told to turn it down, but loud enough so that if anyone wants me they have to come to my room and open the door, instead of just hollering up the stairs. It will always be easier for the person who wants you to take out the trash to do it himself than climb three flights of stairs to tell you to do it. I learned this trick from Quills.

I sat down at my desk, turned on my computer, fished

77

around in my top drawer for my rebus notebook. All the thoughts in my head were jostling for attention like how the little kindergartners at my school push to be first in line. It's quite possible that in addition to scoring low on all those tests, my brain had been burned to a crisp and I would now be unable to keep one thought straight.

I made a list:

IM Reggie and tell him about Jordan's identity theft and Dwight's murder: Was there a connection?
IM Hannah about going to the water park on Saturday.
Work on my Boston Tea Party report.
Consider dreadlocks.

But just as I typed in Reggie's screen name, I lost the will to IM. There was so much to say, and the truth is, IMing is only good for when you don't really have anything to say.

Yesterday my favorite cousin had gotten arrested by mistake, and today I'd seen my first murder victim. It didn't feel right to write those things. So I called Reggie and told him to meet me, something I hadn't done since about fifth grade, when we were open best friends. Reggie loved conspiracy theories, and I had a feeling I had one on my hands.

I ran downstairs, fetched Jupiter from his cage in the living room behind the baby grand piano no one ever played. Mark Clark was involved in a loud computer battle on EverQuest. I told the back of his head that I was taking Jupiter out for some air. Sometimes I worry that Mark Clark will become so addicted to EQ that Quills will have to be the permanent BIC. A frightening thought.

I met Reggie at the playground of Holy Family, where we went to school (one more year, rah!). Holy Family was K–8, so even though we were in middle school and were too mature for the plastic slide and swinging bridge, we still had to put up with it. We had to put up with lectures from our principal, Mr. French, about not splashing in puddles or spitting rocks, like we even did that stupid stuff anymore.

Even though it was nearly six o'clock, the sky was still bright as noon. A few boys in baggy satin shorts were shooting hoops, and a lady was throwing a tennis ball for her yellow lab puppy. Reggie was skateboarding around the play structure.

After giving Reg some grief about not coming after me when I took my double freak show fall off DDR at Tilt, I told him everything, from walking home and getting picked up by Jordan to Dwight's murder.

At the mention of Jordan's name he started warbling, "I am sixteen! Going on seventeen!" in a high girly voice and executing some dancerish spins on his skateboard while flapping his hands in mock dainty fashion. "I know that I'm nigheeeve! Blah blah blah blah, blah yadda de da, and blah blah da da da!" Reggie never missed a chance to tease me about my acting debut as the weepy Louisa in *The Sound of Music*, or in this case, tease Jordan. "Sixteen Going on Seventeen," was, of course, her big dorky solo. Reggie had been very impressed at the time, but we don't talk about that.

"At first it really didn't seem like such a big thing," I said, ignoring his *American Idol* moment. "Someone was arrested and gave the cops Jordan's name, but it's all been worked out. The cops know it wasn't her. But who was it, then? And don't you think it's weird that Jordan and I stopped at Under the Covers and saw Dwight and the next morning he winds up murdered? Don't you think that's too big of a coincidence for it to be a coincidence?"

Reggie listened with his head down, flipping the end of his skateboard up with his toe. At least I think he was listening. It was hard to tell with boys. Finally he said, "Do they have any idea who murdered that Dwight guy?"

"They didn't seem to. They were just going about

their normal detective-type business. Isn't it usually someone you know, when you get murdered I mean?" The thought freaked me out a little.

Reggie looked up from under his bangs and shook his hair a little. Reggie secretly thought he looked like Paul McCartney before the Sergeant Pepper period, and he sort of did. "Maybe she did it."

"She, Jordan? You think my cousin killed Dwight the bookstore guy?" This was something I hadn't considered. I was too busy recovering from being electrocuted and taking all those stupid tests and drawing my self-portrait to ponder this: On the same morning Dwight was killed, Jordan and Tiffani showed up at Casa Clark to pick up Jordan's car. But they came over when . . . about eleven o'clock? Under the Covers opens at ten o'clock, which would have given Jordan plenty of time to stop at the bookstore beforehand.

"But her car was parked at our house," I said aloud.

"You didn't say she ran him over, did you?" asked Reggie, confused.

"Huh?"

"Why would it matter where her car was?"

"How would she have gotten there, to Under the Covers to kill Dwight?"

"Well, the last time I looked, our fair city had a most excellent public transportation system," said Reggie.

"You think she took the bus to commit a murder?"

Reggie shrugged. "Makes more sense than risking having a witness spot your car and maybe writing down your license plate number."

I sat down on the pavement. I felt inside my pocket for Jupiter, who was in his "off" mode, snoring like a big tired cat. I rolled my lips against each other. They were chapped. It was impossible, wasn't it? Jordan took the bus to Under the Covers, then called Tiffani after she murdered Dwight and asked to be picked up at the crime scene? No way. Then I remembered: Tiffani's family lived only four or five blocks from Broadway, on 28th and Thompson. Jordan could have easily walked. I felt cold all of a sudden. I tried to force the realization into my head, but it just wouldn't go.

I changed the subject instead. "Oh, I was electrocuted last night, too." I didn't tell him the part about seeing Dr. Lozano and the tests I scored so low on.

"I thought maybe you'd just forgotten to comb your hair," said Reggie.

I ran my fingers up under my hair. It was snarled underneath like always. I pulled it all up and tied it in a knot on top of my head. "I'm thinking maybe I'll go for dreads."

Reggie laughed and flipped his board. It clattered to the pavement. "Right."

I thought, *At least I don't go around thinking I look like the young Paul McCartney.* "But why would Jordan do it? Doesn't she have to have a motive? Maybe Dwight stole Jordan's identity and she found out."

"Technically, she didn't have her identity stolen. Someone—maybe even a guy—said they were her to get out of having to go to court. But real ID theft is when someone gathers enough info about you to open credit cards in your name so they can buy a bunch of stuff and then you're stuck paying for it."

I looked over at him. Reggie was one of those people who knew a little about a lot of things.

"But Dwight's a guy . . . Wouldn't the cops go, 'Uh, you don't look like any high school girl I've ever seen—' "

Reggie and I looked at each other at the same time. "Jordan could also be a guy's name—" he said.

"Dwight could have gotten arrested and said his name was Jordan and no one would have thought that was weird at all."

Reggie hopped on his board and did a few kick flips. I could tell he was getting bored.

"So maybe Jordan knew all along that Dwight had stolen her identity, and she came back to confront him and . . . what . . . killed him? Isn't that a little psycho?" I knew there were teen murderers in our city. Every once in a while a picture of one in his orange jumpsuit turned up in the newspaper. But this was my cousin Jordan we were talking about. She was too tidy to be a murderer. Though she did have a temper. I remembered the way she screamed at that dumb kid with the skateboard crossing the street before we got pulled over.

"But you got to ask yourself," said Reggie, doing a few fancy flip turns, "why do we care? I mean, the cops will figure it out."

I reached into my pocket and put my hand next to Jupiter. I could feel his heart beating in my palm. Why did I care so much? Because it seemed important. Because caring made life suddenly pretty interesting. Because it was like a rebus come to life.

At the other end of the playground two girls had entered the gate and were walking toward us. One of them was Sarah Schumacker, secretly known as Skanky Sarah Schumacker or S Cubed. She was one of the ultrapopular girls, who, in a movie, would be filmed walking down the main hallway in slow motion. S Cubed had had her own cell phone in fifth grade, when she also started shaving her legs. We wear uniforms at our school—navy blue T-shirts and khakis, which most of us get on sale at the Gap. But S Cubed always wore ultra-low-rise khakis that she got sent home for about once a week because you could see her crack when she bent over in class to pick up her pencil.

In the past I'd been intimidated by S Cubed. She had that ultrafakey nice way of saying, "I really like your *braces*," but everyone knows braces are still braces, even if you have kiwi green elastics and straight teeth beneath all that metal.

As I watched her and one of her cling-on friends stroll towards us, I saw her reach into her purse—it was pink vinyl and said SWEET 'N' VICIOUS on it—and fumble for a cigarette, which she quickly lit before she reached us.

Normally, I'd be nervous coming face-to-face with someone as popular as S Cubed. I'd wonder whether what I was wearing was too stupid, or whether I had a zit on my chin, or if I was having a bad hair day. But now I wasn't thinking about any of that. Instead, for the first time I saw that S Cubed was trying too hard. She wanted to impress us. She was desperate to get her Marlboro Light into her mouth and lit before she reached us.

"Hey, look, it's Reggie and Minerva," she said to her cling-on, then blew smoke through her nose dramatically. "You guys make the cutest couple."

"We're not a couple," mumbled Reggie. Was he blushing?

"Hi, Sarah," I said. "We were just talking."

"How sweet," she said.

"Not as sweet as you trying to impress us with that cancer stick." The words just hopped out of my mouth as if they had lives of their own. "What are you doing that for? Everyone on earth knows it'll kill you."

S Cubed's cling-on giggled.

Then, at that moment, a cell phone trilled from someone's back pocket. Reggie reached for his, and Sarah and her cling-on each dug for theirs in their bags. The ringing continued, and it finally occurred to me that maybe it was my Emergencies Only phone: I'd never heard it ring before.

It was Mark Clark, calling me home, pronto. Two detectives had shown up at the front door, looking for me.

At home, everyone was sitting in the living room. No one ever sits in the living room, except at Christmas, and that's only because the presents are in there. I don't know why they call it the "living" room when no one does any real living in it.

There was no smell of a Mark Clark dinner coming from the kitchen. There was that same smell of aftershave from Under the Covers. That's because Too Much Aftershave with his pale psycho eyes was standing in the living room, waiting to talk to me. Even though I hadn't done anything I felt I was beyond in trouble.

Morgan sat on the sofa with his finger between the pages of a book. Mark Clark stood at the mantel in his business-casual clothes, arranging the cheap little statues of Buddha that Morgan collected and displayed there. Quills sat at the grand piano with his back to the keyboard.

The tall policeman with the army haircut and too much aftershave from Under the Covers introduced himself as Detective Peech. He was a giant. His arm was thicker than my leg. His leg was thicker than my body. The Latino cop with the amazing white teeth was his partner. I didn't get his name. My internal organs were elbowing each other around in there, eager to get out of this doomed body and find a better home. Detective Peech and White Teeth both wore serious suits, like Charlie wears on days he's going to court.

"Here's Minerva," said Mark Clark. He used his stern "this is my baby sister" voice. Mark Clark wore his Paid Assassin Look, but I couldn't tell who it was directed at. Not the enormous Detective Peech, probably.

"That's an unusual name," said Detective Peech. Like he was one to talk. He grinned in that fakey nice way. His teeth were very straight but kind of gray. It was obvious he had not flossed his teeth properly when he'd had braces. Then he said, "You were in the bookstore today looking for a book you'd ordered. You said a woman called and told you the book was in. Did she tell you her name?"

Crap.

"No."

"What did she say when she called?"

I've watched a million reruns of *Law & Order* with Quills, who is an addict. We always yell at those television meatheads who lie to the cops and think they can get away with it. Don't they watch reruns of *Law & Order* and know you can never get away with it? I glanced over at Quills, who was pulling on his bottom lip, staring at me. I bet he was thinking, "Minerva, don't be like those television meatheads."

So I told Detective Peech the truth. I said that no one called me. That I just made it up on the spot because I'd never seen a dead body before and I knew they'd kick me out if they didn't think I was there for a reason. "In a way, I guess I stole that real estate book, because you just handed it over to me and I left without paying for it. Should I go get it? Sir?"

Detective Peech wrote this down in his little note-book. I was not about to say that the day before I had been at Under the Covers with my favorite cousin, who probably had had her identity stolen by the victim and was possibly a teen murderer because of it.

White Teeth crossed his arms and said, "So there was no woman who called you from the store telling you your book was ready."

Didn't I just say that? "No, sir. I made it up."

"It's not a good plan to lie to the police," said Detective Peech.

"I'm telling you the truth now, aren't I?" I am not one for back talking. It only gets you in more trouble. Giving tone is another thing entirely.

"Do you recognize this gentleman?" Detective Peech reached into his coat pocket and pulled out a picture. It was the homeless guy with the orange bandana and the three-legged dog.

Before I could speak up, White Teeth's cell phone rang. My brothers and I all sat and watched while he put the phone to his ear and nodded his head, then said "Uh-huh," then nodded, then said, "Uh-huh."

He snapped his cell shut, made too much of opening his sports coat and dropping the phone into the inside pocket. He had the same look on his face Reggie gets sometimes during an algebra test, when he's the first one finished. I guessed that meant they'd either arrested someone, or they had a pretty strong lead.

Then, as if by magic, White Teeth clapped Detective Peech on his bull-sized shoulder and said, "I think we're done here for now."

- 8 -

THE NEXT DAY WAS SATURDAY. The brothers and I sat at the big dining room table eating one of Mark Clark's humongous German pancakes with lemon and powdered sugar. I don't normally read the newspaper except the comics, but I had a world event report due that required cutting out an article from the newspaper and gluing it to a piece of notebook paper.

Youjustme

Just between you and me, I don't know (a) why we can't print something from the Internet, (b) why it has to be cut from the newspaper and glued to a piece of notebook paper, and (c) how cutting and gluing teaches you anything about world events, since no one actually reads the article, except the headline.

I found an article about mad cow disease and was just about to cut it out when I spied a small story at the bottom of the page that got both my legs bouncing like mad:

Homeless man arrested in bookshop clerk's murder

Portland police arrested a 49-year-old homeless man, Clyde Bishop, in connection with the
murder of Dwight Paskovich, 28, assistant manager of Under the Covers bookshop on Broadway
Avenue. Bishop was apprehended late Friday
night at a parking lot near the bookshop. The
motive appears to be robbery. Officials would
not release details of the homicide case pend-
ing Bishop's arraignment.

I got the chills, remembering how I'd walked past Clyde Bishop and stopped to pet his dog, and how he'd reached out suddenly and I'd thought he was going to grab my ankle. He had given me a friendly, slightly mad look. Who knew it was a robbery-and-murder-planning look?

Except there was something weird about this. What was it? I put down my fork. I bounced my legs madly. Something just wasn't right about this.

"Min, I forgot the syrup. Could you get it?" asked Mark Clark.

"Could you nab the orange juice, too?" asked Morgan.

"Oh, and while you're in the kitchen, could you just give the floor a quick mopping?" said Quills.

"I think there's something wrong with the garbage disposal, too. Want to take a peek under the sink while you're there?" said Mark Clark.

"Doesn't the entire sink need to be replaced, come to think of it?" said Quills.

This old joke never failed to crack the brothers up. They'd ask me for a simple favor—get someone a fork, close a window, pick up my books off the table—and they'd keep adding bigger and bigger "favors" until finally I was replacing the roof on the house or digging a hole for an in-ground swimming pool all by myself. Har!

Normally, I laughed along with the joke, but I just stared at Mark Clark for a minute; then, without saying a word, I went to the kitchen for the Log Cabin. Back in the dining room, I stood just inside the door, my fingers hooked through the bottle's handle. I closed my eyes, trying to remember what I'd seen at the crime scene.

Dwight's head was sticking out from behind the counter, his face turned toward the bookshelves behind the counter. I'd clearly seen the wound, which meant it was on . . . I turned my head slightly, trying to conjure up the image of Dwight . . . the *left* side of his head. That meant Clyde Bishop would have had to hit him using his right hand, right?

"Minerva?" said Mark Clark. "You okay?"

"Could you stand up a minute?" I asked.

Mark Clark wiped his mouth with his napkin and stood up. Slowly, I swung the syrup bottle up toward the left side of his head, the only side that made sense, given that I'm right-handed. To hit Mark Clark on the right side was impossibly awkward; I'd have to cross the front of my body, and I wouldn't be able to even reach the right side unless he turned his head at the last minute. But Dwight's wound was on the left. I was sure of it. And I was sure that for Clyde Bishop to clock someone in the head hard enough to kill him, he'd need to be right-handed, too. But wasn't Clyde's right hand his useless, shriveled hand?

"Earth to Minerva," said Quills.

Morgan scoffed. *"Earth to Minerva?* Soon you'll be saying 'groovy.'"

"I already say 'groovy,'" said Quills. "It's ironic."

They yakked for a while about this, but I wasn't listening. I handed Mark Clark the syrup and sat back down. I wasn't hungry.

I reread the newspaper article aloud.

Quills said the true tragedy was that Clyde Bishop probably killed Dwight just to get cash to buy some cheap red wine. Morgan said, "Well, if that made it easier for the guy to get through the night, then whatever."

I said, "But it happened in the morning. In broad daylight!" What did Morgan know? He wasn't *there*. I was there. I was there, and so was Detective Peech and all those other detectives, and I was pretty sure they had arrested the wrong guy.

"It's an expression," said Morgan. "Whatever gets you through the night."

"Oh," I said.

He reached over and patted my head. I hated when he did that. I took my plate into the kitchen and let it clatter in the sink. It was a pink-and-blue plastic plate with Jasmine from *Aladdin* on it in her stupid harem pants and big cow-eyed look. Why did my brothers still think this was my plate? It was a stupid baby plate. I took it outside and threw it in the garbage can.

On Saturday mornings I was supposed to clean my room. I shoved everything that would fit under the bed and took all the clothes on the floor and stuffed them into the laundry chute at the end of the hall.

I tried to stop thinking about Clyde Bishop and his

wilted flower hand cradled in his lap. I sat on the edge of my desk chair and flipped open my rebus notebook.

I made this one:

ban ana

Banana split. It wasn't one of my better ones.

Weirdly, I was excited about going to the water park. I didn't care that I had to wear the extra long red Speedo with the yellow flowers. It was just a swimsuit, and it didn't have Baby Elmo or Simba on it or anything. It did have that horrible shelf-bra thing, but, what do you know, now my boobs filled it out pretty well, and I didn't think I looked dorky at all. *And* it was still too long! I had to keep pulling at the waist so the leg holes wouldn't droop around the top of my thighs. I wanted to tell my mom, "*Ha*! See, I didn't grow!" But of course my mom was in Santa Fe, teaching yoga. I tried not to feel too sad about that. Instead, I thought about the next bathing suit I would get, which would be a two-piece with board shorts.

When Quills dropped me at the water park on his way to work, Hannah and Julia were already there, hanging on the snack counter, waiting for Devon-or-Evan to show up. The park smelled strongly of chlorine and steamed hot dogs. It was crowded with kids holding big presents, all arriving for birthday parties. We were too old to have birthday parties here now.

"Minerva," shrieked Julia. "Hannah said you weren't coming!" Julia had bigger brown cow eyes than the Jasmine on my plastic plate.

"Really?" I thought I'd told Hannah I was coming, that I'd only said "no way" in my head. Anyway, here I was. I just couldn't pass up that steep red slide that shot into the deep end.

"Hey, Minerva," said Hannah. "How ya doing?" She came over and slung her arm over my shoulder. She wore a blue flowered bikini top and matching board shorts. "Should I get a cookie? They have awesome chocolate chip cookies here. Or will it go straight to my ass?"

I stood back and looked at Hannah. I did not think the chocolate chip cookie would go straight to her ass, because that just wasn't possible, but I did notice her shorts looked tight. "I don't know. But if your stomach's full it will make your shorts feel even tighter."

Hannah made a show of shoving me away. "Like you're one to talk!"

"I'm not the one asking about eating a cookie," I said.

Hannah tucked her black hair behind her ears carefully. Hannah was beautiful. Her mom was from Thailand. Her hair hung down the middle of her back like a satiny cloak. I used to spend a lot of time thinking about what it would be like to have that hair, but now I liked my hair. You could stick a pencil in it and it would *stay in.*

Julia giggled. "Minerva, you're supposed to say, 'But, Hannah, your ass is so perfect, you don't need to worry about cookies!'"

"Yeah yeah yeah. Whatever," I said.

We stood at the snack counter for about three weeks, but no one showed up. We made jokes about how we could just reach around the side of the Plexiglas box on the counter and take as many cookies as we wanted. Probably, if Quills were there, he would do that, just to see what happened. Hannah insisted that Devon-or-Evan worked on Saturdays. She'd even called and checked.

But the person who finally came out of the back room was a girl with a name tag on that said Sam. She wore her hair slicked back in a high ponytail and an irritated expression. Her expression was so irritated it put Hannah off from asking if Devon-or-Evan was even working.

Julia and I ordered a slice of cheese pizza and a Pepsi. Hannah wanted a hot dog and was stuck waiting while Ponytail Girl steamed one up for her. Julia and I went to nab a table before they were all taken.

The huge wave pool had been turned off, like they always do between open swim sessions, so the lifeguards can check to see whether there were any dead bodies drifting around the bottom, or to see if any little kids may have pooped.

"So who do you think will get elected Rose Festival Queen?" asked Julia, taking a sip of her drink. I'd forgotten that Julia's sister, Alison, was also on the Rose Festival Court.

"No clue," I said.

"Probably not your poor cousin. I feel so sorry for her!"

"It turned out to be no big deal," I said. They had the worst cheese pizza here, greasy roof-of-the-mouth burning cheese on cardboard.

"You mean they're going to give Jordan the Hightower Scholarship after all? Alison said the committee or whoever decided to give it to Zoe McBride. Do you know Zoe? Her little sister is in my tae kwon do class."

"What are you talking about?" I tried to take a bite, but dropped the cardboard wedge back on the plate.

"You didn't hear?" said Julia. "Alison said the people who give out the Hightower did a background check on Jordan or something and found out she'd been picked up by the cops. So they took it away and gave it to the second girl in line. Zoe."

The Hightower Scholarship was a big famous scholarship awarded every year to one senior girl in the state to go to the college of her choice. She could go anywhere in the country, and she got a full ride. The girl was always a fine young woman who got straight A's and excelled in a sport. It was a huge deal. I know about it because Morgan's girlfriend got it a couple years ago, decided to go to Brown over on the other side of the country, and kicked Morgan to the curb before she even got moved into the dorm. Or that's Morgan's heartbroken version anyway. I knew Jordan was going to go to Stanford. Or wasn't going, if what Julia said was true. Jordan's dad had departed the scene when Jordan was little, and her mom, my aunt Susie, had two jobs. I doubted Jordan would be able to go to college without the Hightower.

"But that's so unfair. Jordan didn't even do anything. The arrest was a mistake." I wasn't going to tell Julia that the thought had crossed my mind that my favorite cousin might be a teen murderer.

"They probably don't even like that it *looks* as if she's done something wrong. There are tons of other girls who applied for the scholarship who didn't get arrested, by mistake or *not* by mistake. Know what I mean?" said Julia.

"I was there. The cop took her in, but it was someone else who'd been arrested and gave them Jordan's name." I explained how identity theft worked, but I could tell Julia wasn't listening. I saw how it was with people. In sixth grade we learned that in a court of law you're innocent until proven guilty. But in the minds of every-day people, just having had the bad luck to be mistakenly arrested made you guilty of something. It was so unfair.

"So what's with you today?" asked Julia out of the blue.

"With me? I don't know. This pizza sucks." I'd taken off my hoodie and jeans and piled them on an empty chair. This stupid Speedo wasn't too bad. I still had my purple high tops on, since walking around barefoot at this place was a sure recipe for athlete's foot.

"I don't know," she said. "You seem different."

"I was electrocuted at Mark Clark's art opening on Thursday night," I said.

"I thought people, like, died from being electro-cuted," she said.

"Yeah, I say electrocuted, but I mean electric shock. I was shocked, that's all."

"Well, yeah, it would be shocking," said Julia, then laughed at her own joke.

Then Hannah showed up with her hot dog, took my clothes off the empty chair, and dropped them on the floor.

"That's really kind of a hideous bathing suit," she said to me. "As your friend, I'm just trying to be honest."

"Yeah? As your friend I'm telling you that's pretty crappy, talking to a friend like that. Just being honest." I pushed the leg of Hannah's chair with my foot. "When did you get so mean?" I asked her, point-blank.

Hannah giggled, as if I'd said something funny. Then she shrugged, ripped off a piece of the spongy hot dog bun, and stuck it in her mouth. "If you could change one thing about yourself, what would it be?"

The Change Game was an old game we've played since forever. You say what physical feature you'd change and why. So, for example, I'd say, "I'd change my nose because it looks like a turnip." Then you'd say what famous person's nose you'd rather have instead. The game keeps going until you can't find one thing left to change. It's like Monopoly, though, because like Monopoly, the Change Game can go on and on. In all the years Hannah and I have played it, we've never run out of things we'd change about ourselves.

Hannah started and said she'd change that little dip between her nose and her upper lip.

"It's called a philtrum," I said.

"Well, whatever," said Hannah. What was her problem? Maybe she was irritated because Devon-or-Evan wasn't around. "Maybe we should start with you, Minerva. Since you probably have bigger things you'd like to change than your *philtrum*."

Julia giggled. "I'll go," she said. "I'd change how my eyes are uneven. Have you noticed how one is higher than the other? I'm like, who's that painter guy, Picasso. I'm like one of his paintings. Instead, I'd like eyes like Michelle Branch."

"She's so over," said Hannah.

"But she still has gorgeous eyes," argued Julia.

Had this game always been so lame? And boring? Julia knew she had gorgeous eyes. Even Sister Patrice, the crabby nun with the huge ears who ran the computer lab at school and who thought we were all Satan's spawn, remarked upon Julia's beautiful eyes.

I sighed. I saw the lifeguards retake their seats and put their whistles in their mouths, which meant they were about to turn the wave machine back on. I stood up. I wanted to check out an inner tube before they were all gone. There was already a long line in front of the equipment booth. Which to tell the truth I did not mind standing in. Suddenly, there was so much to think about. Was Jordan really going to lose the Hightower Scholarship because of this mix-up, or was Julia just "embellishing"—the word Mark Clark said meant dressing up the truth to the point where it was a lie? And what about poor Dwight? And now, poor Clyde Bishop, with his wilted lily hand, sitting in jail for Dwight's murder? And wasn't it all somehow related? I couldn't help thinking it was. But how?

I knew one thing for sure: If Jordan lost the Hightower

she was sunk. She'd be stuck here in Portland doing I don't know what. All college was expensive these days. Even I knew that.

"What about you, Minerva?" said Julia.

"What about me, what?" I said.

"What's the first thing you'd change about yourself?"

"Uh . . ." My mind went blank. "I don't know."

"If I was Minerva, I'd say my legs. How can they be both fat and skinny at the same time?" Hannah laughed.

"Or my arms. They're kind of gorillalike. My knuckles practically drag on the ground, have you noticed?" said Julia.

"I think I'd change my hair. It's really . . . thick . . . but kind of in a witchy way," said Hannah, pulling her beautiful satiny hair up and out to the sides of her head.

"What about those little blackheads on the end of her nose?" said Julia.

"And what about the nose itself?" said Hannah. "What about the nostrils?"

Now they were just picking anything. I could see that. It had become a game on top of the original game: Pick on Minerva Clark. Normally, I would have just sucked it up. But I could tell that what used to be considered normal in my life had changed.

"What does this do for you, saying stuff like that? Make you feel more hot and gorgeous? It's pathetic. All it does is shout out loud and clear how insecure you are."

Once again, Hannah giggled for no reason. Julia, who was about three degrees less cruel than Hannah, busied herself with taking the plastic lid off her Pepsi and poking at the ice with her straw.

I stood up and bent over to search my jeans pocket for money for the inner tube. It must have been then that Hannah and Julia figured out that my red Speedo didn't really fit me, that it was too long. I heard them whispering behind me, but I just ignored it. What could I do?

I went to stand in the line in front of the equipment room. The line was long, snaking all the way past the lap pool. My face felt hot. I hated it when Hannah and Julia made fun of me, and they'd been doing it in their sneaky awful way since we were in first grade and I was about eight feet taller than everyone else. But underneath my hurt feelings was that weird calm feeling.

If Mark Clark were there, he would try to tell me that Hannah and Julia were just jealous, but they weren't. They were both hot and they knew it. But maybe they were jealous of something else: that I didn't care about their game anymore.

I finally reached the head of the line and laid my dollar on the counter outside the equipment room.

"Sorry, we're all out," said the inner tube giver-outer.

He turned sideways a little so I could see there was nothing left in the equipment room but a pile of broken lane markers and a few deflated tubes. At first I thought he was at least Morgan's age, because he was at least as tall as Morgan, but I could tell he didn't shave. He had that crunchy green-brown hair that swimmers get from too much chlorine and eyes as blue as a mountain lake. His name tag said Kevin.

"Oh no!" I said. No inner tubes? I wanted so badly to float around in the wave pool, to have an excuse not to talk to Hannah and Julia.

He looked down at me, his thick eyebrows pressed together. "Maybe there's one back here that's not so flat that I can pump up."

"I don't mean to sound like some freak," I said. "I was just counting on an inner tube. Floating around helps me think and stuff, you know?"

"You have stuff to think about, do you?" Kevin had picked up one of the deflated black tubes and was feeling around the edge to see how bad the damage was.

"Yeah, actually. I do."

Kevin dropped the inner tube and looked at me. I looked straight into those mountain-lake blue eyes. He smiled right at me. My brothers smile right at me all the time, but it wasn't like this. Kevin didn't have braces, but he had a retainer.

As if from far away, a cell phone rang. Kevin reached into the pocket of his shorts and pulled out his phone. I noticed there were red flames on the faceplate. This could have been my cue to wander off, but I stood there like a meathead.

"Yep . . . got it . . . yep . . . you got it . . ." He looked at me and rolled his eyes. "You'll be here at six o'clock. All right. Good luck in your fight against evil, Toxic Avenger." He snapped his phone shut. "It was my mom," he said, although he didn't have to.

"Your mom fights evil?" I asked, laughing.

"She thinks she does. She works at U.S. Bank in the fraud division."

I must have looked blank.

"You know," he continued, "catching people stealing debit cards and stuff."

"Like identity theft and stuff?"

"Yeah, exactly like that." Kevin grinned, surprised I knew what he was talking about. We looked at each other until I felt the old campfire start to burn in my cheeks. I guess that was one thing that hadn't changed: the ability to get embarrassed when a hot boy looked me straight in the eye.

"It's okay about the inner tube," I said.

"If someone turns one in early, I'll set it aside for ya."

"Okay. Cool."

Suddenly, Hannah and Julia were standing on either side of me. It was so fun talking to Kevin I hadn't been paying attention. I was surprised when Hannah cocked her head to one side and purred, "Hey, Kevin."

"We thought your name was Devon!" said Julia.

"I did *not*," said Hannah.

"She wants to know why you haven't called her," said Julia.

"What*ever*," said Hannah. I could tell she was embarrassed. Hannah made a face at Julia, and I thought it was because she wanted Julia to shut up.

I looked at Kevin and he shrugged. It dawned on me then—d'oh!—that Kevin, *my* Kevin, was Hannah's Devon-or-Evan. He'd obviously been moved from the snack counter to the equipment room.

"Come on, Min, we want to apologize for making you feel bad," said Hannah, her hand on my arm, guiding me away from Kevin and the equipment booth, and back past the pool deck to our table. I turned back to look at Kevin, but he was already talking to the kid who'd been in line behind me.

"We really are sorry," said Julia.

About halfway back to the table Julia suddenly dropped her arm around my shoulder and Hannah slipped her arm around my waist, just above my hip. They shoved me between them a little, almost like they wanted to play London Bridge and they were doing the "take the key and lock her up" part.

It happened in a heartbeat: Julia tugged me back against Hannah's arm, and I felt them both grab the too loose sides of my too long Speedo, then yank up as hard as they could.

I'd been ambushed and wedgied. And this was not just any wedgie, but the biggest wedgie in the history of the water park. No little kid shooting off the slide and hitting the water butt first had ever experienced a wedgie as big as this one. It was my extra long, too loose Speedo, all that extra fabric that allowed for maximum wedgification. I have brothers. I grew up giving and getting wedgies. This one was massive, a 10.0 on the wedgie scale.

I felt a sudden, unmistakable chill on my bare buns. I reached back and felt skin, up to my armpits, I swear. I could not believe I was able to walk. I could not believe Hannah and Julia had not completely cut me in half. The campfire was roaring in my cheeks. I thought of my white butt, with its birthmark that looks like Cuba, out there for everyone to see. I didn't dare turn around to see if Kevin was watching. I prayed to the guardian angel of seventh-grade girls that he was still talking to that kid. What could I do but try to put things right the best I could? I reached back with the pointer fingers of each hand and pulled the leg holes of my bathing suit back to where they should be.

Hannah and Julia had scampered madly back to the table. They were screeching and sobbing, grabbing their stomachs and making a big stupid show of practically falling out of their chairs.

"It was a joke!" said Julia when I reached the table.

Hannah opened her mouth, but before she could tell me not to get mad, or whatever she was about to say to convince me that she was just a nice, fun girl who liked a good laugh, her cell phone rang from inside her Sponge Bob backpack.

I recognized the ring. It was the same ring Jordan's phone had, the same ring I'd been anxious to stop the day I answered it while she was outside being arrested.

Hannah answered it and her face went through a few expressions in about two seconds: dimply happy to eyebrows raised in surprise to frowny mad. She thrust the phone at me.

"It's for you."

I sat back down. "Hello?"

"You need new friends." The voice was familiar. I looked over at the equipment booth and saw Kevin on his cell phone. He pointed at me and grinned.

"He's right," I said to no one in particular.

Then I did something that cheered me right up: I

snapped Hannah's phone shut, drew my arm back. As I said, I have brothers. I can throw farther than any girl I know. I lobbed her metallic-pink phone high over the heads of all the screaming kids and parents splashing around. It briefly caught the light streaming in through the windows before plunging into the deep end of the lap pool.

By the time Hannah's mom picked us up a few hours later, it was pouring. She was the quietest mom of all the moms I knew, since she didn't speak the best English. It was raining so hard that Hannah's mom had to have the wipers on extra high. *Thwap! Thwap! Thwap!* It was so irritating. The whole day had turned out irritating, except for how nice Kevin was to me.

Hannah and Julia were not my best friends. Usually, when we were driven somewhere we all smooshed together in the backseat and made the same old jokes about being chauffeured around. Today Hannah and Julia got in the backseat and made me sit in the front. I probably had it coming for throwing Hannah's cell phone in the pool. I was surprised how *not* in trouble I got. Hannah merely shrieked, "That is so uncool." She even had to dive down to the bottom and get it herself. Ha!

Thwap, thwap, thwap. The wipers were loud enough

to hide their whispers. It didn't bother me much. They could whisper all they wanted, but nothing would take away that perfect moment when Kevin called Hannah's number and asked for *me*.

Still, something bothered me about Kevin's phone call. There was a silver of time after he spoke and before I recognized his voice when I had gotten a fizz of fear. Fear of what? Then, suddenly, a few things occurred to me all at once, like the way you can't find your favorite jeans, hoodies, and toe socks, and it turns out they've all been together in the clothes dryer.

I cracked my knuckles madly, which I knew was not good for the health of my joints, as Mark Clark told me whenever he caught me doing it. The call reminded me of answering the phone in Jordan's car. It reminded me of talking to Quills's friend Toc. I remembered how angry he sounded. And Toc was a sneaky guy. Look at the scam he showed Reggie and me at Tilt, how you could trick the change machine into thinking a Xeroxed five-dollar bill was a real five-dollar bill. That was sort of like identity theft. The same person who'd think of tricking a change machine might also think of tricking a cop by giving him someone else's name. But what did Dwight have to do with it? Maybe he found out that Toc had given the cops Jordan's name? But was that worth killing somebody over? Maybe Dwight was going to turn

Toc in, and Toc was just going to talk to him and didn't mean to kill him.

There were too many questions.

Then I thought of Kevin and his nice blue eyes and shiny swimmer's hair and I thought maybe Toc thought Jordan was hot. Maybe he wanted to hook up with her. Maybe he knew that if he got her in trouble with the law, she'd lose the Hightower and she'd be forced to stay in Portland. Maybe he didn't want her to leave.

My poor joints. I did another round of mad knuckle cracking. I remembered that it was Saturday evening, the night the Humongous Bag of Cashews liked to practice, and they were practicing in our basement. Toc was probably already at Casa Clark, plugging in his guitar and testing his amp. Little did he know he had some explaining to do.

-9-

HaNNaH'S MOM PULLED UP TO CaSa Clark and I got out and thanked her for the ride. Hannah and Julia waved from the backseat and said, "See you at school," just as if nothing had happened. Maybe they were afraid if they complained about the phone, I'd bust them about giving me a massive wedgie.

Inside, I went straight to the living room and scooped Jupiter up from his hammock inside his cage. I could hear the TV on upstairs. I took the steps two at a time up to the TV room, where Morgan and Mark Clark were sitting on the Cat Pee Couch. Before we got Jupiter we had a fat tabby named Elroy who'd stroll past your legs and spray them, so that you'd leap up, disgusted, and he could steal the warm spot where you'd been sitting.

Morgan and Mark Clark were watching *The Matrix* and drinking Mountain Dew. When no one can think of anything else to do in this house, they watch *The Matrix* and drink Mountain Dew. A cookie sheet piled high with nachos sat on the coffee table. They would never be able to get away with eating nachos off a cookie sheet if Mom were still around.

Mark Clark asked me how the water park was. He really was a pretty good older brother/parent substitute. I said it was okay, because I didn't feel like telling him about Hannah and Julia, the wedgie, the flying cell phone, and how a hot boy that Hannah wanted to hook up with had been nice to me instead. I really didn't want to tell that part about Kevin, because Mark Clark liked to make jokes about my first boyfriend and how the dude was going to have to get past my three big brothers first.

For some reason, I also didn't want to mention what Julia had heard about Jordan losing the Hightower Scholarship on account of her identity theft.

"Are the Cashews practicing tonight?" I asked.

"Yup," said Morgan, without looking away from the TV. Even though he'd seen *The Matrix* eight million times, he hated to be interrupted.

It was the part in the movie where the Morpheus character offers Keanu Reeves the red pill or the blue pill. The red pill will lead Keanu to the truth, and the blue pill will allow him to go back into his life in the Matrix as if nothing had ever happened.

From two floors down I heard the complaining twang of a guitar, then the beginning of scales. Toc, Quills, and the two other guys whose names I always forgot were already in the basement warming up.

Suddenly, I felt all jittery anxious. I pressed my fingers against my eyes to calm myself. They smelled like chlorine. I knew how Keanu felt. I could either take the blue pill and go upstairs and turn on my music loud but not too loud and IM with Reggie about nothing and work on my rebuses, or I could take the red pill and go downstairs and face Toc. I tried not to think that Toc might also have killed Dwight. I didn't like thinking we had another teen killer around, this one my brother's best friend.

After another loud twang or two, I started for the basement.

Does anyone ever really choose the blue pill?

On the way downstairs I stopped in the kitchen and snuck a piece of Top Ramen. When it's uncooked it's like a big fat king-sized cracker. I get in trouble for eating raw Ramen, mostly because no one knows what to do with the little packet of seasoning that's always left over. Sometimes, I throw it away, even though it's wasteful. I ate a slab of Ramen and drank milk straight from the carton. I was going to need my strength.

I was also going to need to look at Toc the same way I'd looked at S Cubed that day at the playground, when I saw, for the first time, that when I stopped obsessing about how people were looking at me, I could really look at them. I really *saw* S Cubed then. I saw how she tried too hard. I saw how she was eager to impress Reggie and me. I saw that she cared too much what we thought about her.

I wiped my hands on my pants and took a deep breath. I felt sure if I could just get a good long look at Toc's face, I would know if he was guilty.

Going into the basement to listen to Humongous Bag of Cashews practice is not something I would normally do. Our basement was big, but not big enough to hold a whole rock band and their equipment comfortably. If you wanted to listen, you had to sit on the washing machine.

I could feel my pulse in my ears as I tiptoed downstairs. Why was I tiptoeing? I tried to walk normal. Toc and Quills were going over some chords when I appeared. They barely looked up. The drummer looked over at me, then went back to playing his air drums.

I realized I couldn't just stop practice and say, "Hey, Toc, did you steal my favorite cousin's identity, then murder Dwight at the bookstore for reasons I have yet to figure out?"

I went and sat on the washing machine. Unfortunately, someone was doing a load, and the spin cycle jiggled my bum. I stared hard at the back of Toc's head as he bent over his guitar, his long white fingers crawling up and down the neck. He'd changed his one-on-top-of-the-other double ponytail for two pigtails on top of his head. He wore jean cutoffs and a blue sweatshirt that said LIFE IS GOOD on the back.

Toc went back to his spot in front of the drums, struck his lead guitarist rock star pose, with his feet apart and his head tossed back, and started yelling/ singing something about how his girl was so expensive it was time she was made to pay. Humongous Bag of Cashews covered a lot of Nirvana and Pearl Jam, but they were always working on their own songs, and this was one of them.

And then he looked right at me and said, in the same voice he'd used on the phone that day, "You robbed my heart blind. Don't think I won't make you pay. I will nickel you. I will dime you. Nickel and dime you. To death."

I stared right back at him, even though I was jiggling along with the dryer. He was just practicing that bad dude rock 'n' roll look on me. I'd never noticed Toc had a unibrow.

I waited until they took a break. The other guitar

player collected money from Quills and Toc and went to make a Burger King run.

On TV it looked so easy when investigators cornered possible suspects. What was I going to say?

"So what was your motivation for writing that song?"

"Which song would that be, Minnie Mouse?" Did he have to call me that? He drained his can of Red Bull and started rolling a cigarette on top of one of the amplifiers.

" 'Nickel and Dime You,' " said Quills.

Toc laughed. "That would be the difficulty dealing with your gender."

"Anyone I might know? Like my cousin Jordan?"

Quills went *Woot*! And the drummer hit his cymbals with his sticks.

Toc stopped rolling his cigarette and stared at me. This was not his bad dude rocker look, but something else. His eyes flicked down just for a second. Then he put on a phony grin and grabbed his chest. "Ah! Jordan Parrish! Be still my heart! You are far far too good for the likes of this poor musician!"

I said, "You're not supposed to smoke in here."

"Really? What're you going to do about it, Minnie Mouse?" He licked the paper, dabbing at it with his pointy pink snake tongue.

I had no clue what I was going to do about it. What was I going to do about any of this? I was in seventh grade. I wasn't Detective Peech. I couldn't just flash my badge. I was his friend's little sister. The best I could do would be to back talk a little and see what happened.

"I don't know, maybe steal your identity. Like what happened to Jordan."

"Steal my identity? Whooooooo." He made the haunted house sound and pretended to be all scared.

"Did you hear about the guy at Under the Covers? Dwight? He was murdered."

"*That* guy," said Toc. He sat down on the little blue chair that used to be my desk chair and crossed his legs high up on his thigh. He jiggled his foot, slapped his flip-flop against the sole. Nervous. "That dude was into some seriously nefarious stuff."

"Like Xeroxing five-dollar bills and fooling change machines?"

Toc laughed and blew smoke up at the ceiling. He jiggled his foot some more, slapped his flip-flops. "Who do you think taught me that trick?"

"Dwight?" I said stupidly.

"Nah, my older brother. But ol' Dwighty taught it to him. They were in the same Boy Scout troop back in the day."

"And Dwight taught your brother the trick with the five-dollar bill and the change machines, and your brother taught you," I said. I understood exactly what he meant, but I was trying to figure out what to say next. I could just say, "Oh, cool," and hie myself back upstairs, but then I flashed on the sight of Dwight playing with Jupiter and telling me about the origins of the word "ferret." No, I was sure I was on to something, I just didn't know what.

"Why are you so curious? Don't you have some Hilary Duff movie to go watch or something?"

"I knew Dwight," I said. "He was a friend."

"Then you certainly know he was up to some seriously nefarious stuff at that dumb bookstore."

"Yeah, so," I said. I had to be careful. I had no clue what Toc was talking about. The washing machine's spin cycle had stopped. I drummed my heels against the side of the machine. I liked the dull metal bong.

"So? *So?* Man, you are one harsh chick, Minnie Mouse. How would you like to be one of those poor old grannies?"

Huh? Poor old grannies? Which poor old grannies were we talking about here?

"I wouldn't," I said.

"I mean there you are, like, about ninety years old, and you go to the same little bookstore you've gone to since forever, and you're not hip to the debit card thing—you don't even know what it is—and nice ol' Dwighty happily takes your check—so many places don't even *take* checks these days—and the minute you leave the shop with your book about knitting or cats or whatever, nice ol' Dwighty copies your checking account number and goes to one of those check-printing places and gives them your checking account number and whatever name he wants. The checks are printed in a matter of days and he's got a couple of weeks to write as many checks as he wants before the POG gets her bank statement."

"What's a POG?" I asked.

Toc shrieked and clapped his hands. "I knew you were BSing me! You had no idea your buddy Dwight was such a crook. POG! POG! Poor old granny!"

"What are you talking about?" I said. It wasn't a question. I had tone in my voice. I was the tone *queen* all of a sudden. Was he saying Dwight was some kind of an identity thief himself? That he would basically steal the checking account numbers of his customers and write checks on their accounts until they ran out of money or got their monthly statement? We'd done a section of social studies on personal finance, and we'd had to go to the bank to open our own checking accounts.

"I'm only telling you what my brother told me," said Toc. "You could buy the biggest flat-panel plasma HDTV on the planet and be long gone before the POG even had a clue." He was waggling his eyebrows and smashing out his cigarette on the concrete floor. He picked up his guitar, stuck it next to his amp, and delivered that thick loud reverb that Mark Clark is always saying ruins your hearing.

I hopped off the washer and ran upstairs. Jupiter twisted and turned inside my pocket, as anxious as I was to get out of there.

- 10 -

I PULLED JUPITER OUT OF MY pocket and held him to my chest. He wriggled around and tried to bite me in the thin spot between my thumb and pointer finger. He didn't like it when I took the stairs two at a time. I didn't like to jostle Jupiter, but this was totally urgent.

Mark Clark and Morgan were still flopped on Cat Pee Couch, watching *The Matrix*. The only way you could tell time had passed was that most of the nachos were gone, and Morgan had crushed the middle of his empty Mountain Dew can and snapped it onto the bottom of his shoe.

"I need to call Jordan," I said.

"Okay," said Mark Clark.

"I mean, I need her number."

They sat there as if I hadn't said a word. I then did something for which I would get yelled at: I stood in front of the TV and put my hands on my hips, so they couldn't see around me.

"Hey! This is the good part," said Morgan.

"You can always rewind it," I said. "It's not like *The Matrix* is going to suddenly cease to exist—"

"Watch the tone," said Mark Clark.

Morgan dug in his pocket for his cell phone. He flipped it open and tapped around with his thumb.

"Not in here. Sorry."

He was hardly even looking. What was it with these guys? It's so true what Ms. Dayton-Bunnsted said, that girls are the superior gender.

"Why do you need to talk to Jordan?" asked Mark Clark.

I was *so* not going to go into it. I bet they didn't even know that Jordan was on the verge of losing the Hightower Scholarship and probably wasn't even going to get to go to college. Her entire future was probably ruined. And the guy responsible was in our basement at that very moment, singing a song about how he was going to get back at her.

I stomped back downstairs and returned Jupiter to his cage behind the grand piano. He looked at me with his little white face. *Why aren't we going to play now?* Sorry, Jupiter. Suddenly my life had gotten more complicated.

In the kitchen there was a desk where everyone piled all the papers they didn't know what to do with, junk mail, and catalogs. No one ever went near the pile, because even breathing on it would send the top papers sliding to the floor, and then you'd be the one who had to clean it up. Behind the pile sat a phone and a Rolodex address file. My aunt Susie's was probably in there somewhere.

I carefully leaned my body into the pile of paper and slowly reached over it to grab the Rolodex. As I stood up a few envelopes slid off the top; I hoped it wasn't the beginning of an avalanche. I'd seen about a million avalanches on the Discovery Channel when I was little.

I was lucky. No paper avalanche, which meant no explaining why I was snooping around. I thumbed through the Rolodex. Did Aunt Susie have a different last name than Jordan? I couldn't remember. Suddenly I felt freaked-out nervous. What if Quills or Toc came upstairs? Or Mark Clark or Morgan came downstairs? Or the drummer came back with the burgers? They'd ask me what I was doing. What *was* I doing?

There was only one Susie in Mom's Rolodex. I picked up the phone and dialed the number.

"The number you have reached is no longer in service. Please check the number and dial again."

Crap.

I stood in the middle of the kitchen, chewing on my thumbnail. I was always trying to stop biting my nails and always failing, especially when I started feeling ultrastressed.

How hard could it be to get ahold of my own cousin?

I glanced through the kitchen door into the dining room and saw a gray work jacket slung over the back of one of the dining room chairs. I stared at the bulge in one of the pockets. That was Toc's jacket, and I crossed all the fingers I could that the bulge was Toc's cell phone. I knew he had to have Jordan's number in his directory somewhere.

I ninja crept into the dining room, listening for sounds from the house. Upstairs, the TV. Downstairs, a short drum riff, then laughter. The sun was getting ready to drop behind the west hills and it blasted light through the windows, blinding me. I reached into Toc's pocket—yes!—and pulled out his phone.

I pressed the Menu button (which has always troubled me; why is it called Menu when there is no food involved?), found Incoming Calls—no, I didn't think Jordan would be calling him, would she?—then found Outgoing Calls, pressed through a short list until I came upon the call Toc had made that day I'd answered her phone.

Reggie told me once that seven digits—the number of

numbers in a phone number—is the maximum amount a human can remember without having to write it down. I stared at Jordan's number, made a song of it in my head, dropped Toc's phone back in his jacket pocket, then walked through the dining room, into the front hallway, and up the stairs, taking them only one at a time, calmly, like it was a fire drill at school.

At my desk I wrote the number down quick on the back of an old math assignment.

Then I IMed Reggie.

Ferretluver: OMG, you won't believe the weird stuff going on around here.

BorntobeBored: Not as weird as here. My mom is teaching me to do *laundry*.

Ferretluver: Listen I gotta talk to you.

BorntobeBored: It's part of her Philosophy of Independence. I don't wanna wash a bunch of stinky clothes. Nasty!

Ferretluver: Did you see in the paper where the cops arrested that homeless guy for Dwight's murder?????

BorntobeBored: So it wasn't your cousin after all?

Ferretluver: NO. But I'm pretty sure it wasn't the guy they arrested, either. I think Toc has something to do with it. The day Jordan got arrested I answered her cell phone by mistake and he told her—I mean me—that she better watch out, because he's going to get her.

BorntobeBored: And that relates to Dwight's murder how?

Ferretluver: I don't know. It turns out Toc actually *knows* Dwight—through his older brother. And he also knew that Dwight was stealing check numbers from customers, then using the numbers to print new checks.

BorntobeBored: I've heard of that scam—you think I'm guilty, too?

Ferretluver: Maybe. Are ya?

BorntobeBored: So what do you have on Toc?

Ferretluver: He's mad at Jordan for some reason. He knew Dwight. He knew Dwight's scam. And he thinks nothing of doing scams himself. And he wrote this really creepy song for the band that's about getting back at someone. It was kind of drama queeny, I thought—the song that is—but whatever.

BorntobeBored: I dunno. Something's missing. Where was he the day Dwight was murdered?

Ferretluver: I dunno =(I probably should find out, huh? Also, where was he the day the person who was arrested gave the cops Jordan's name instead of his own? It was Valentine's Day, Jordan said.

BorntobeBored: Argh—BRB—gotta go sort the whites.

Ferretluver: Do you think I should talk to Jordan? Tell her what I know? Oh!!!! Julia said she might be losing the Hightower because of the arrest.

BorntobeBored: Julia. There's a reliable source. BRB.

Next to my room on the third floor is a small study under the slanty part of the roof. There's nothing in it but a red leather chair, a bookcase full of old books Charlie had in college, and a tiny table with a phone. No one ever used this room except Morgan, when he was in his I'm-going-to-be-a-poet phase. No one ever remembered there was a phone in there. I sat in the red leather chair and thought about what I was going to say.

I dialed Jordan's number. The phone rang twice, then went to voice mail.

"Jordan, hi, it's me, Minerva Clark. I've got something really important to tell you. My friend Julia told me about the Hightower. Did you really lose it, or was that just Julia embellishing? Julia's sister is Alison, you know, from the Rose Festival Court. *Anyway,* it's about Toc, you know from my brother's band, well, of course you know. Anyway, I have some information about him that you might like to know, so please call me back. Oh, it's Minerva Clark. I guess I said that. Well, er, bye now."

Crap. That could have gone better. Reggie was right. Something was missing here, something big.

Do I need to say that Jordan didn't call me back? I tried to tell myself it was because I didn't leave our home phone number, but the real reason, of course, was that I sounded like a dork. This sleuthing business wasn't as easy as they made it look on *Law & Order*. Of course, those were grown-ups who'd gone to crime-solving school, and not seventh graders with active imaginations.

I stayed in my room with my rebus notebook open on my desk until Mark Clark called me down for dinner. I took the fire pole straight down to the kitchen, something I hadn't done since fifth grade. The house was quiet. Humongous Bag of Cashews had finished practicing, and Morgan had gone out somewhere. It was me and Mark Clark and my mom's mac and cheese, baked with black olives and mushrooms.

I wished my mom was around. She would eye me and ask me what was going on. Moms always know when something is going on. I don't know how they do that. I would tell her that I'd discovered, all on my own, that Toc was responsible for Jordan's losing her scholarship, and maybe even murder, and she would tell me not to be a Nosy Parker. I would wonder what a Nosy Parker was, and she'd tell me some long story about when she was a girl growing up in California, and I would be sorry I'd asked.

Instead, Mark Clark dished up our plates and we went upstairs to the TV room. Since it was Saturday, we were allowed to eat in front of the TV, and I was allowed to drink soda instead of milk or juice, which were my beverage selections during the week.

Mark Clark popped in *Finding Nemo*. My brother still thought I watched cartoons. He didn't know that the last time I spent the night at Hannah's we'd watched *Troy*, and saw Brad Pitt's naked bootie. Hannah's mom let us watch it because even though it was rated R, we convinced her that we were studying the Trojan War in history.

"So did you manage to get ahold of Jordan?"

I looked over at him, staring at the TV, fast-forwarding through all the dumb previews, trying to see if he knew more than he was saying. "Nah," I said.

"I'm sure you'll hear from her eventually. From what I hear, this Rose Festival thing is keeping her pretty busy."

From what I hear? What had Mark Clark heard?
"Yeah," I said.

"You okay?" He looked over at me.

"What's with her and Toc?" I blurted out, fishing for I didn't know what.

Mark Clark laughed. "Nothing, I don't think. He'd like there to be something. What guy wouldn't. If Jordan Parrish weren't my cousin . . ."

Was he serious? I couldn't imagine poor Mark Clark with any girlfriend, much less someone as hot as our cousin Jordan. But I guess when you're a guy, you have to say stuff like that.

Then the movie started, and we were saved from having to discuss it anymore. I sat Indian-style on the Cat Pee Couch and thought about what Mark Clark had said about Jordan being busy with the Rose Festival. It seemed to me that everywhere you looked there was always some princess showing up at some concert or art opening or air show or softball game. I don't know what they did there, other than stand around in their stupid tiaras looking like the hottest girls in town, but in the months of May and June, they seemed to be everywhere.

Which gave me an idea.

I said I needed to go to the bathroom. Morgan's room was at the end of the hall next to the second-floor bathroom. As boys' rooms go, it wasn't too awful. There were some clothes in a heap in the corner, but otherwise he was the neatest one of all of us. He had that famous black-and-white poster of Albert Einstein sticking out his tongue over his water bed, which was perfectly made with a dark green-and-blue plaid comforter.

I sat down at his computer, which I knew was always online, and quickly Googled Rose Festival Court. After smiling pictures of all the ambassadors in identical red V-neck dresses and strands of pearls, there was a calendar of their activities.

I was in luck. The very next day, Sunday, at eleven o'clock, at the Civic Auditorium, was the dress rehearsal for the queen's coronation.

I scampered back to the TV room, where Mark Clark was looking very sad that Nemo was lost.

The next morning was sunny, the sky clean and blue. I was relieved; somehow it was easier to sneak around in good weather. I'd tried to get Reggie to come with me, but his parents were taking him to a blues festival or something. Sometimes I felt bad for Reggie. In a way it was better having no parents to speak of than parents breathing down your neck day and night, trying to broaden your horizons.

As I tied the laces of my purple Chuck Taylors I wondered how, exactly, I was going to get past whatever brothers happened to be around, get downtown to the Civic Auditorium, and back before anyone knew I was missing. I decided the best plan was not to make too big a deal about it. I turned some music on and closed my door.

It turned out to be so easy I started thinking that maybe I should be more worried about being kidnapped from my third-floor bedroom than I normally was. Quills was gone when I got up—Sunday was his full day at Kinko's—and after breakfast Morgan went somewhere on his mountain bike, leaving the back door wide open. Mark Clark was on EverQuest. His hair was sticking up all over the place; he hadn't even combed it. Some big battle was going on or something, because when I stood behind him and said, "I'm going to meet Reggie," he didn't say, "Where are you meeting him?" or "Be back in a half hour," or anything.

Instead, he yelled at the computer, "I could use some help here!"

Some lizardy-looking monster was killing him pretty good, I guess.

"So be back in a bit," I said.

"It's about time!" he yelled again, bouncing up out of his chair, then typing something like a madman.

This was the advantage of living with all boys. They never listened.

I was pretty sure I knew how to get to the Civic Auditorium because in sixth grade we'd taken a field trip to see *Poe! Poe! Poe!*, a totally depressing play about Edgar Allan Poe. It meant walking about a half mile to the MAX station, then taking the light-rail downtown. I half expected Quills to roar up next to me in the Electric Matador and ask me what in the hell I thought I was doing. I'd never taken the light-rail by myself before. My stomach was a little jittery until I got on and found a seat. I noticed that everyone was reading a book except a bum wearing a greasy red parka and a knit cap. I wondered if people thought maybe I was a runaway, since I didn't have a book.

I got off the light-rail at somewhere downtownish looking. There were big office buildings that looked old, made of brick with white pillars. The courthouse maybe, or City Hall. I couldn't really tell. I was starting to sweat in my Vans sweatshirt. Starbucks seemed like a safe place to go into for directions. The barista dude making the lattes said, "A couple blocks that way and a couple blocks that way," and flung his hand back behind his ear.

I went down one block and over one block and over one block, asking at every Starbucks along the way until I found it. But by then it was almost one o'clock. The dress rehearsal had started at eleven o'clock. It looked as if it was over by now. There was a long row of glass doors across the front. I jiggled the handle on one door after another. All locked. The box office was shut tight, with a small square of wood placed over the hole where they pass you the tickets. I looked inside, through the lobby, and the doors to the auditorium itself were all closed.

Suddenly, I felt really far from home, like the way I felt when I was five and Charlie accidentally forgot me at the grocery store. Except now there was no friendly check-out lady to rescue me as I stood crying in the soups and noodles aisle. It also occurred to me that I should have brought Jupiter—I'd never go out to meet Reggie without Jupiter. And what if Reggie called while I was gone? Mark Clark would say, "I thought she was with you!" I could only hope that Mark Clark wasn't paying any attention when I went out.

Just as I was going to turn around and retrace my steps to the light-rail, I heard two girls' voices. I spun around. Jordan emerged from the door at the other end of the building. She was carrying a lavender dress inside a plastic bag like the kind you get at the dry cleaners, and a pair of green beauty-pageant high heels. She was wearing a cool black leather jacket and tapping some numbers into a tiny silver cell phone. She was talking to someone behind her as she walked. Then Tiffani came out.

Beneath her leather jacket, which looked pretty dang new, Jordan wore a yellow tee with Cookie Monster on it. Tiffani wore the same tee, only hers had a picture of a cowboy on it. Jordan's shiny light brown hair was stuck up on her head in a messy bun and so was Tiffani's. Jordan had about three inches of skinny rubber bracelets marching up her bony arm and so did Tiffani. Before, I'd always thought they were just best friends who liked the same things, but now it looked to me as if Tiffani was really a cling-on.

"I just can't do it," said Jordan. "I don't know how else to tell you, okay?" She stomped ahead of Tiffani, the dress over her arm flapping against her legs. I'd never seen Jordan so angry. Even when she'd gotten arrested by mistake she wasn't this mad. She also had purple circles under her eyes. I guess being a Rose Festival ambassador is more exhausting than it looks.

Tiffani trotted along beside her, trying to keep up. "You know, I really thought you were way cooler than this," she said.

Jordan opened her mouth, then abruptly closed it when she saw me standing there. "Minerva. What's up?" She was not glad to see me.

"Hey," I said. As usual, I didn't know how to begin. I shoved my hands in my pockets. "I heard about the

Hightower. That's really sucky. Are they really going to take it away from you?"

"Who told *you*?" said Tiffani. She said it like I was just some stupid little kid who didn't have the right to know anything.

"My friend Julia's older sister is on the court," I said.

"It looks like it," Jordan said. "They're still deciding." She pulled her brows together, then looked off across the street at the fountain, a collection of big concrete blocks with waterfalls gushing over each block. She had tears in her eyes but a hard look to her mouth, as if she was determined not to cry. I remembered the weeks during *The Sound of Music* when she'd brought me a PayDay every day. For some reason, that got me more than anything else, that she always took time to stop and get us candy bars.

"Jordan," I said, putting my hand on her arm. "What is going *on*? I mean, I mean . . . you heard about Dwight, right?" It was one of those times when you launch into a sentence and it's like going down a too-big hill on your skateboard; you push off and realize you don't want to be going down this big hill at all, so you hop off before you pick up too much speed. If for some weird reason Jordan didn't know her friend was dead already, I did *not* want to be the one to tell her.

"I heard about it," she said softly, dabbing at the tears

that threatened to spill onto her cheeks with one knuckle. Then she released a huge, tired sigh.

"It was on the front page of the paper," said Tiffani. "And they caught the guy anyway."

"But he was your friend," I pressed, ignoring Tiffani. I was not going to say that no, they didn't have the guy, that it was *impossible* for Clyde Bishop with his useless, shriveled-up right arm to have murdered Dwight. "Don't you think it's bizarre that first you were arrested by mistake and the very next day a friend of yours was murdered? A false arrest and then a murder? Have you ever known anyone who's been murdered?"

"He wasn't a friend," said Jordan. The tears tipped out of her eyes and flowed down her face, smudging her black mascara. "He was just someone I knew."

"Still, Jordan. He was murdered."

"I know, I know, I know!" She started crying harder. I could tell she was telling the truth. She reached up to wipe her eyes, realized she still had the lavender dress in the plastic cleaners bag slung over her forearm, tried to shift it to the other arm, but dropped it. She stooped to pick it up, then hung her head and sobbed. A guy walking by in a suit and—what do you call those hats Jewish men wear? a yarmulke—called over, "Is everything all right over there?"

"We're fine!" yelled Tiffani.

The man waved and walked on.

"I just don't know why everyone's *on* me!" sobbed Jordan.

"No one's on you," I said.

Tiffani snorted. "Oh gosh, Minerva. First there's a mistaken arrest, then Doug from the bookstore is murdered, then Jordan is told she might not get the Hightower, then her psycho seventh-grade cousin turns into a junior stalker."

I stared so hard at Tiffani I thought my eyes would pop out of my head from the strain. "What are you *talking* about?"

"What are you doing here, Minerva?" asked Tiffani. She bent down to collect Jordan's dress and help her to her feet.

"His name's Dwight, not Doug," said Jordan.

I thought, *Okay, okay, forget Dwight for a minute* (as if). I needed to remember why I was here: to tell Jordan my suspicions about Toc, who had it in for her. I didn't have concrete proof yet that he'd given the police her name, but I was sure enough to warn her to be careful. *That's* why I was here!

So I started in. I told Jordan I thought it was unfair that someone got away with giving her name to the cops, not just unfair, but weird, really. I mean, why *her* name? If someone wanted to avoid getting arrested, why didn't they just give some random name? Why Jordan Parrish? It wasn't like Sarah Jones or Jennifer Smith, which sound fake, but also probably belong to dozens of real girls.

Obviously, it was someone who knew her, someone who knew she'd gotten the Hightower Scholarship and knew she'd lose it when it came out that she'd been hauled down to the police station. I didn't know if this was true at all, but it sounded good. It sounded *serious*, and what I really wanted was for her to take this seriously and to watch her back. "Someone has it in for you," I said.

"Someone else has been watching too much TV," said Tiffani, laughing and rearranging her bracelets. Jordan laughed, too, but it was just something to do. She wasn't amused at all.

"And I started thinking about it, and I think you should watch out for Toc," I said. "You know my brother's friend Toc?"

"And he's going to do what to her?" asked Tiffani.

This was a good question. I felt the sun beating down on the top of my head. Did I really think Toc was going to murder Jordan? If he had murdered Dwight, surely he was capable of murdering my cousin, too.

"I just think that if Toc did something creepy and against the law like stealing your identity, that he might do other stuff. I asked him where he was on Valentine's

Day"—this was a pure lie, but I could see that Jordan had calmed down and was starting to look around a little; she was losing interest. "That was the day the person who got arrested gave the cops your name, remember? I asked Toc where he was, and he got this really weird look on his face. I could tell he'd been up to something."

Jordan sighed. She took her hair out of its messy bun and stuck it back up again. She was all done crying, and suddenly she was mad. It was like accidentally stepping on the tines of a rake hidden in long grass—*blam*, right between the eyes.

"You know, Minerva, Tiffani's right. I don't know what little girl Nancy Drew bull you think you're pulling here, but you don't know anything, okay? And I don't need you snooping around in my life. I'm fine with the way things have turned out. Just do me a favor and stay out of it.

"And for your information, Toc was with *me* on Valentine's Day, so he couldn't have been the one to mess up my life. Got it? In fact, if you want to get technical, I'm the one totally responsible for all the crap that's come raining down on my head. It's my own fault! Got it?" Her face had gone from white to red. She pushed past me and rushed away, the plastic bag holding her fancy dress flapping against her legs.

Tiffani started after her, then on second thought

stopped and put her hand on my shoulder. "Don't feel bad, Min. She's just really upset."

I turned to watch as Tiffani ran and caught up with her friend. I didn't know what to think, except that now I'd have to find my own way home. I'd somehow counted on Jordan being so grateful that she'd offer me a ride.

- 11 -

WHEN I GOT HOME QUILLS WAS standing in the middle of the kitchen pulling on the ends of his crayon-yellow blond hair and having a full-on hissy fit. *Quills.* The cool brother. What was Quills doing home? Wasn't he supposed to be at work? Uh-oh. Mark Clark was leaning against the counter with his arms folded across his business-casual polo shirt (even though it was Sunday, Mark Clark always dressed in business casual) telling him to relax.

I came in the back door. I could have snuck past the kitchen and fled upstairs, but I knew Mark Clark and Quills were arguing about me and where the hell I was, and I would be in even more trouble if I ran and hid in my room, so I walked right into the kitchen.

"Where were you!" yelled Quills. "What's up with you? Where's your head at, little girl! First you just take off from Tilt. Now you just leave the house!" He was bouncing up and down on the balls of his feet like a madman. There was spit in the corner of his mouth.

"I told Mark Clark," I said. "He was playing EQ." That was code for, I could have told him I was going to set my hair on fire and jump off a bridge, and he would have said, "Have a good time."

"You said you were going to meet Reggie," said Mark Clark. "And that was"—he turned his wrist over and looked at his watch—"three hours ago."

"This is seriously uncool of you," said Quills. "Seriously uncool."

"I thought you were at work," I said.

"I got off early," he yelled. "And it's a good thing, too, since no one else seems to be minding the fort!"

Minding the fort? What fort? Was this more of Quills being ironic?

I stood there.

They stood there.

What was hanging in the air, of course, was that they shouldn't have to be dealing with me, that this was parent business.

"Where were you, anyway?" said Mark Clark.

"It's just going to make you madder," I said.

145

"If you were out doing drugs or getting into some kind of trouble that's just going to come back and bite all of us in the butt, you'd better tell us now," said Quills. He tugged at the hair behind his ear so hard I thought he was going to pull it out of his head.

For a second I thought about saying, "Darn, caught me!" but this clearly wasn't the time to break out the attitude.

"I went to meet Jordan. That's why I wanted her phone number yesterday, remember?"

"Jordan our cousin?" Quills asked, as if he'd never heard of such a thing.

"No, Michael Jordan," I said. I couldn't help it.

"You're in enough trouble as it is, dude. I'd watch the back talk," said Mark Clark.

Dude? Mark Clark was calling me *dude.* Maybe I was just on the verge of hysteria, but I started to smile. I stared down at the linoleum so he wouldn't see it.

Then Mark Clark clicked into lecture mode. I got a long speech about how even though I was in seventh grade and felt all grown up, I wasn't all grown up and I couldn't just come and go as I pleased. But the worst thing I did was lie about where I was going, because if I started lying, then they'd never believe me again, and it was important that we trusted each other.

I kept staring down at the floor. There was something

mashed into the linoleum that could have been either a piece of mushroom that fell off a pizza or a really icky bug. I tuned in to Mark Clark now and then to see if he'd gotten to my punishment yet. Finally, he said the worst words you can say in our house: dish duty.

My head snapped up. "Dish duty? But why?"

"I just told you why. Weren't you listening?"

"Yes," I said. *No.*

"You are lucky it's only for a week," said Quills. He stomped out of the room, then marched right back in. "Oh, wait! All this rage has made me really thirsty!" He got out a glass, filled it halfway up with water, drank half, then tossed the rest in the sink. "Minerva, dishes," he said, then stalked out for good.

I would rather be grounded to my room for a month than do dish duty, which my brothers knew. Even though we had this huge house, I *lived* in my room. I loved my room, with its ferret posters and white shutters and high four-poster bed. I didn't have a TV in my room, but I had my computer. Make me stay in my room for a week! See what I cared!

But dish duty was the pits. Dish duty meant cleaning up after three evil boys. And on the weeks I was punished with dish duty, they were extra evil. Mark Clark would make complicated dinners that used every pot and pan we owned. Morgan, who snacked on Cap'n

Crunch and usually rinsed out a single bowl and spoon and put it on the windowsill for the next time, would get a fresh bowl out of the cupboard every single time. Quills—who'd had more dish duty growing up than either of the other brothers—was the worst. When Humongous Bag of Cashews practiced and someone went out for the usual Carl's Jr. run, Quills would make them all eat off plates. He'd even dump each individual bag of french fries onto a plate.

There were dirty dishes from the time I got up until the time I went to bed. It was the same as being grounded, only with lemon-fresh Joy. I hated my brothers. Why couldn't I just have a normal mom who yelled a couple of mean things, then cried because she worried she was wrecking my self-esteem?

I ignored Quills's dirty water glass *and* the cookie sheet from yesterday's nachos, still propped against the side of the sink, and stomped upstairs myself.

Ferretluver: So after I got SLAMMED with dish duty for telling the bros I was with YOU, Mark C. said you called?

Borntobebored: Wahn-wah. Sor-ry.

Ferretluver: What about the blues festival?

BorntobeBored: Haven't left yet. Hey! Ya got to check out MontgomeryHighChat.com.

Ferretluver: I went to find Jordan to tell her that I think my bro's creepazoid friend Toc was probably the one who stole her identity, but she just ripped into me. I think she and Toc are an item. Or were an item.

Borntobebored: Maybe it wasn't Toc. Maybe it was whoever posted this flame. Unless it was you who posted it! :\

Ferretluver: ME?? Why would I post it?

Borntobebored: Cuz yer cous was being a biatch! And you just trying to help her find out who's messin wit her.

Ferretluver: I don't even know what site yer talking about. I'll have to check it out. Anyway, we gotta work on our Boston Tea Party report.

Borntobebored: I'd rather pin my hand to a burning log with a dull fork!

I linked to MontgomeryHighChat, and sure enough, someone had flamed Jordan:

QT_PIE865:
I for one am relieved that it's payback time for hootchie suck-up queen Jordan Parrish. Those of us who pay attention know what a poseur she is. And now she lost her big scholarship. Boo-hoo. It's about time people got wise to that biatch.

I logged off. My head hurt. My brain was exhausted big-time from all this thinking. I thought everyone liked Jordan, and I mean really liked her. Not like with Chelsea de Guzman, where people said they liked her, just so she wouldn't start some mean vicious totally untrue rumor about you. Jordan was nice to people like cling-on Pansy Burrows.

I took my rebus notebook out of my desk drawer and flopped down on my bed. I didn't feel much like puzzling out rebuses these days. I looked through all the ones I'd made so far. I tossed my notebook across the room.

Why had Jordan yelled at me like that? What had I done to make her so mad?

An odd feeling stirred inside my chest. I sort of missed the old Minerva Clark, who worried endlessly about being a Gigantor or having hair that was too thick and not silky enough, not straight enough or curly enough, who thought endlessly about how she looked like a dorkazoid with her braces, that her boobs were too flat and her butt was too big. If I was that girl again, I would be too worried about how I looked all the time to get caught up in a mystery that was getting messier by the day. It was like how I sometimes secretly missed playing with my stuffed animals. Life felt safer then, predictable.

I opened my closet door and scrounged around the pile of ugly clothes that always seemed to wind up off the hanger and on the floor. Maybe if I found something really horrible, it would stir the spirit of the old Minerva.

I found a pleated pink (pink!) skirt Nana Clark had bought at the Goodwill. Nana Clark loved the Goodwill. The skirt had little pockets on the hip with kittens (kittens!) embroidered on it. I found the matching white top with pink sleeves and a pink chest pocket with yet another kitten embroidered on it. I pulled the shirt over my head and struggled into the skirt. It had a side zipper that zipped only halfway. I hadn't even checked myself out yet, but I could tell I wouldn't feel any self-hatred. All I thought was, *What a stupid, cheap skirt.*

I looked at myself in the mirror for a long time.

Hey, pretty in pink, just like the movie title said.

I spent the next hour going through all the ugly clothes I could find: puff-sleeved blouses and T-shirt dresses, long skirts with matching belts, a plaid hat like Scottish people wear. I finally dragged out the most awful dress ever made: a bright yellow dress with a scoop neck and an A-line skirt that I wore to another cousin's wedding last June, where I was forced to be the flower girl. I remember putting on the hideous dress and refusing to leave my room. I cried until my eyes swelled shut. Until that moment, I had never understood why some people wished they'd never been born. I felt like a school bus rambling down the aisle with my stupid basket of rose petals, and more than one person at the reception afterwards had made egg yolk jokes. I put that dress on and stared hard at myself. I turned on the overhead light and stared harder. *If I wore dresses, this one wouldn't be so bad.* Except the color, of course, made me look as if I had a tropical disease.

I crawled back into my RAMONES FOR PRESIDENT T-shirt and khakis and lay on my bed, looking up at the glow-in-the-dark stars that Mark Clark had stuck up there when I was little. No wonder I didn't want to play the Change Game with Hannah and Julia. It wasn't that the game was lame or boring—although it was that, too—it was that I couldn't think of anything I'd change. The voice that told me I was ugly was dead, electrocuted that night at Mark Clark's art opening.

Now I really was a freak. I didn't know one girl at school who thought she was okay just the way she was.

There was a soft knock on the door. Morgan stuck his head in before I could say, "Come in," which I *hate*. His hair was wet from the shower, and his hazel eyes were soft with concern. Morgan was always the peacemaker. Maybe because he was closest to me in age or because he was a Buddhist.

"Hey," he said.

"Hey," I said.

"Whatcha doing?" he asked as he sat on the very edge

of my bed. He cradled something wrapped in a paper towel in his hand.

"Nothing." I wished I had Jupiter there so we could drag him around on a towel or something and not have to have a Moment. I looked outside the window over my bed. The sky was pink with sunset.

"The bros filled me in."

"I bet they did." And people say girls tell each other everything.

"So why'd you sneak out?" he asked.

I sighed. I had a blue-and-yellow *Powerpuff Girls* comforter on my bed, a Christmas present from last year. I traced the outside of Buttercup's big green eye. I was too old for the comforter but not old enough to demand a new one.

"I had information for Jordan that I thought was important. About who'd stolen her identity and made her lose her scholarship."

"She lost her scholarship?" asked Morgan.

"You're not allowed to have an arrest on your record. Even one that's a mistake. Or that's what they say. I guess they haven't decided for sure. I don't know." I crooked my arm over my eyes. I thought about mentioning Dwight's murder, but suddenly I was just too tired.

Morgan considered this. One thing that was good about Morgan, he listened to you as if you were someone

153

he'd hang with. He was never fakey nice, the way some grown-ups were, pretending to find everything you said *entertaining*.

I heard the door open again. I took my arm away from my eyes and saw Quills standing there. He, too, had something wrapped in a piece of paper towel.

"Oh," he said, but then he just stood there.

"What kind of information did you have for Jordan?" asked Morgan.

"I think Toc did it, stole Jordan's identity. I think he wants to mess with her because she broke up with him or something." I looked straight at Quills. I sat up and pulled my knees to my chest. "I know he's your friend and everything, but I think he's got really bad vibes."

"Toc's not a bad guy," said Quills.

I snorted.

"I know he comes off as kind of a jerk sometimes, but it's all an act. There must be kids like that at your school."

I thought of Reggie's friend James, who always wore a tweed newsboy cap at a jaunty angle and wanted everyone to call him JET, his initials. He quoted movie lines and pretended they were his own, even though they were from movies everyone had seen a million times.

"Well, anyway, Jordan says Toc was with her on Valentine's Day—that was the day the person was arrested who said she was her."

Quills laughed. "In his dreams."

"That's what Mark Clark says," I said.

"It's pretty much common knowledge," said Morgan.

"What do you mean?"

"Toc's been hot for Jordan since high school," said Quills. "Remember that New Year's Eve party Mom and Charlie had that one year? He met her then. He was a senior and she was a freshman. But she's so not into him, it's pathetic. We've told him for years to get over it, but the poor guy continues to pine."

"But Jordan said they spent Valentine's Day together."

"I don't think—wait . . ." Quills interrupted himself, then gazed up at the ceiling, thinking. Then he started laughing, his arms crossed over his skinny middle. "Nope, Toc wasn't in town on Valentine's Day. The Cashews had a gig that weekend, I remember. Toc was out of town all week. His mom made the whole family go to the National Square Dancing Convention—in Nebraska or somewhere—Toc comes from a long line of champion square dancers. It's his deepest secret."

A few square dancing jokes came to mind, but I let

them pass. Why had Jordan lied to me? She wasn't into Toc, so why had she said they were together? She was trying to protect him, but she didn't even need to. He wasn't even in town. I tried to remember what her face had looked like when she told me. She was furious, too furious for what was going on, I thought. She'd told me then to mind my own business.

"Anyway, don't worry about Toc. He's a lovesick puppy. That's his main problem. There's no need to stress about it," said Quills.

"I'm not stressing." I *was* stressing. Something was definitely going on.

"So no more sneaking out or snooping around, all right?" said Quills. "Just let this thing go."

"Don't you have some big report due anyway?" said Morgan.

"Boston Tea Party," I said, sighing. "I picked the topic because it had 'party' in the title. I didn't know it was about *taxes*."

"Oh, and this is from Mark Clark." Morgan unwrapped the paper towel. It was a Rice Krispies square.

Quills laughed. He unwrapped *his* paper towel. Another Rice Krispies square.

"Two great minds—" said Quills.

"One great thought," said Morgan.

"Thanks," I said. "I take it there are dishes?"

"Well, d'oh," said Morgan. They laughed and high-fived. There are definitely worse brothers out there.

I didn't say anything else. I wanted them to leave.

After I heard their steps on the stairs I logged back on to MontgomeryHighChat. I reread QT_PIE865's flame more carefully for clues. The Rice Krispies squares sat on their paper towels on the corner of my desk, untouched. Instead, I braided and unbraided big sections of my hair.

Who would call Jordan a hootchie suck-up queen and a biatch? A guy probably. But not Toc. It was clear that Toc had nothing to do with this. He was at the National Square Dancing Convention over Valentine's Day—wait until I told Reggie!—and had had it bad for Jordan since forever.

But what about his knowledge of Dwight's check-cashing scam? Maybe it was just as he said. He knew because his older brother told him. It was so hard to know what was true. Julia had embellished about Jordan losing the Hightower, *if* you believed Jordan. But Jordan had lied about being with Toc, so maybe she was lying about other things, too. Maybe Jordan really wasn't a one-hundred-percent-good person. Maybe she was only an eighty percent good person.

Anyway, someone probably from Montgomery High thought she wasn't even that. They thought she was a biatch. And about eight million people went to Mont-gomery High.

I put my head down on my desk. As I drifted off I thought of another rebus:

2↑set

Too upset.

- 12 -

I UNLOADED THE DISHWASHER AND RELOADED
it with coffee cups, teacups, glasses sticky with Mountain Dew, and a lot of cups and glasses sitting on the
counter that didn't even look dirty. Pots and pans I
had to do by hand. I squirted some lemon Joy on a
sponge and wiped out the square glass dish from the
Rice Krispies squares. I looked out the kitchen window over the sink, but it was dark outside and threw
back my own reflection. The bass line of some song
thumbed through the ceiling; Quills's room was over
the kitchen.

One thing about dish duty, it gave you lots of time to
think.

I had to find out who had posted that flame about

Jordan. I had a sneaking suspicion that whatever he had against Jordan might have something to do with why Jordan lied to me about Toc's being with her on Valentine's Day and with why she had gotten so mad at me. Now that I knew Toc was innocent and that he'd been hooked on her for a while, I could see why she might find me totally annoying for pestering her about him or think I was a stupid middle schooler, or whatever, but she'd been massively pissed off that day. I'd struck a nerve and maybe her flamer knew why.

Maybe, I thought, they had some

busines.

Some unfinished business . . . get it?

I smoothed a red-and-white checked dish towel out on the counter, rinsed out the Top Ramen pot, and laid it on the towel. The obvious way to find out the identity of the flamer was to post to MontgomeryHighChat.com and see if maybe he or she would come out and say who they were, although it was unlikely. And even if they did, I knew only about five people who went to Montgomery High, mostly the older brothers and sisters of my own friends, like Julia's older sister, Alison.

I was in the middle of wiping down the counter when I figured it out.

Mark Clark was sitting at his computer, like usual, but

he wasn't playing EQ. It looked as if he was working on his fractals, or maybe it was businessy stuff.

I sat in the wooden chair next to his desk and sighed loudly.

"What's up?" he said, without looking away from the screen.

"Computer science homework. I kind of forgot about it."

"When's it due?" he said.

"It's extra credit. We're supposed to find out how message boards work. From a computer standpoint, I mean."

"Well, a message board is nothing more than a big database. It's sort of like a chart that holds information in different boxes."

"Uh-huh." I really didn't want Mark Clark to click into lecture mode. "But I mean, take a message board like MontgomeryHighChat. How does the message get from someone's computer onto the board?"

"Everyone's computer has an Internet address called an IP address, which is how your computer talks to anything on the Internet."

"Is the address like a home address? Like, you can look it up somewhere and see whose computer it is?"

"Sure, if you knew how, you could."

"Huh. I bet you know how."

"Well, *yeah*."

We sat. He typed a little. I wagged my foot.

"So, like, how do you find the IP address? Like, if someone posted a flame about you, could you find out who it was or where the flame came from?"

"You could. Or you could just ignore it and walk away." He looked over at me with a raised eyebrow.

"Yeah, but this is for school. It's extra credit, like I said."

"Okay." He pulled up MontgomeryHighChat.com, clicked around the site a bit, then pulled up something called NetworkSolutions.com, then clicked around there a little, then typed, then clicked, then typed some more.

"Man," he said, "the security on the site really sucks. It took me ten seconds to get into the administrative side of this turkey." He sat down deeper in his chair, pushed up his sleeves. Okay, he was into it now.

"Cool," I said. "Then what?"

"Then you look up the user history and it'll give you account information for the user and their IP address, and then you use some network tools—some of which I wrote myself, by the way—"

"—in your hacker days?"

He laughed. "I don't know what you're talking about. Anyway, you use some network tools to look up who the

IP address is registered to in the real world, and if they have any Web pages tied to it or whatnot."

"That's so cool. How about . . ." I pretended to be thinking, "QTPIE865. Try that one."

More typing, more clicking. "Nope, there's nothing."

I tried not to show how disappointed I was. We Clarks never got headaches much, but I had one now.

"Wait, is there an underscore or anything in there?" he asked.

"Maybe. Try QT_PIE865."

"Parker Burrows? Is that someone you know from school? Or I'd bet that's his dad."

No, but I knew Pansy Burrows, Jordan's biggest cling-on and now my number-one suspect.

On Monday morning I had a PowerBar and a banana for breakfast (no dishes). I ate standing in the kitchen studying the calendar stuck to the side of the fridge. There were two weeks and three days left of school. There were no days off except this Thursday, when we were dismissed at noon. The Junior Rose Festival Parade marched down Sandy Boulevard, two blocks from our school. Middle school bands played "Louie Louie," and herds of little kids in tae kwon do clubs and Irish dance teams kicked and leaped their way down the street. The traffic was so bad, no parents could get through to Holy Family to pick up their kids at the normal dismissal time, so we got out early.

That's the day I would go to Montgomery High and implement my plan, which involved tracking down Pansy Burrows. I had some questions for her, questions I hoped would rattle her enough to spill. Pansy Burrows was one of those small, nervous girls who in another life was probably a yappy little dog ladies sometimes carry in their purses. I was confident she'd be easy to crack, but I needed to talk to her face-to-face; it was just too hard to tell if someone was lying over the Internet. Plus, on *Law & Order* the detectives were always just showing up and unnerving their potential subjects. They never, like, called on the phone and said, "Hi, we think you're guilty of murder. Could you come in for a chat?"

On Mondays, Wednesdays, and Fridays we had religion first thing in the morning. In class, Hannah sat in front of Julia and Julia sat in front of me. One or both of them were wearing a new perfume that smelled like pineapple. They each wore identical Happy Bunny bracelets strung with pink plastic beads. The Happy Bunny charm read YOU'RE ICKY. When I asked Hannah about hers, she said it was a private joke with Julia.

"We got them at Claire's on Sunday," said Julia. "You know, the day after you flashed your bootie at Hannah's boyfriend."

"Julia, that's one." Ms. Kettle, our religion teacher,

wrote Julia's name on the board. Ms. Kettle was one of those ladies who could be thirty or could be fifty. She wore polyester pants that sat up under her armpits and reading glasses on a chain around her neck. Julia smirked and turned back around in her seat.

It took me a minute to realize that Julia was talking about Kevin, the nice inner tube giver-outer at the water park. Flashed my bootie? *They* gave *me* a wedgie! Hannah's boyfriend? She didn't even know his name! She'd called him Devon-or-Evan. My stomach felt as if it wanted to fling itself up my throat and out of my body. I clenched my fist around my pencil. I bet Ms. Kettle would do more than write my name on the board if I plunged the point into the back of Julia's neck.

Our lesson that day was on the difference between empathy and sympathy. Empathy is when you know how someone else feels when something sucky happens to them, because the same sucky thing has happened to you. Sympathy is when you feel bad for someone because something sucky has happened to them and you know in your heart it's a sucky thing even though it has never happened to you.

Ms. Kettle made us get into groups of three, where we would then create a skit illustrating either empathy or sympathy. Hannah and Julia turned toward each other. Their third was Lily Contrell, who I knew for a fact

Hannah hated. Lily got straight A's in prealgebra and brought egg salad sandwiches every day for lunch. She always had mayonnaise stains on her T-shirt and terrible gas. I had a lot of empathy for her, having to partner with Hannah and Julia.

Reggie, James, and Ari did a skit about a guy whose skateboard gets run over by a bus. Lauren and the two Chelseas did a skit about a girl who dyed her hair red but forgot to wear gloves, and her hands turned flaming red with the dye. This was empathy for Lauren, apparently (it had happened over the summer), and sympathy for the two Chelseas.

When it was Hannah, Julia, and Lily's turn, Lily leaned over at the waist and fluffed out her dark blond hair, which was as wavy and curly thick as mine. She put her fists in front of her, as if they were in the pocket of a hoodie, and walked up and down in front of the class-room saying, "Have you seen my ferret? Has anyone seen my ferret?"

I understood right away that it was supposed to be me. Ms. Kettle watched Lily drag back and forth across the front of the classroom. It wasn't much of a skit.

"What are you trying to convey, Lily? Are we sup-posed to feel sympathy because you lost your pet?"

Hannah and Julia stood behind Lily and whispered behind their hands.

"She's supposed to be me," I said. I didn't even raise my hand.

"No," Hannah said quickly. "Ms. Kettle's right. Lily lost her pet ferret and we feel sympathy for her."

I glanced over at Reggie, whose hand was in the air. When Ms. Kettle called on him, he said, "I have empathy for both Julia and Hannah for thinking they're funny when they're lame."

The whole class laughed. Julia blushed and Hannah frowned as they took their seats. I muttered, loud enough for them to hear, "How does it feel to be on the receiving end of instant karma?"

Julia spun around and said, "F you, Minerva Clark." She made the massive mistake of letting it fly during a two-second slot of time when no one was acting up, when Ms. Kettle didn't have her back turned to the board, when everyone could hear her loud and clear.

"Julia!" Ms. Kettle roared, not as embarrassed or as shocked as you might think. She pointed at the door. "You're out of here."

Julia quickly walked out of the room without looking at anyone, even Hannah.

Suddenly, something hit me on the shoulder. I looked down and saw a small, triangular-shaped note. The triangle was Reggie's trademark folding style. I leaned down, scooped it up without anyone seeing.

Reggie had written his own rebus:

funny   words
          words
funny   words
          words

Too funny for words.

Tuesday afternoon I came home from school to find Charlie there, home from his business trip to New York. I'd seen pictures of Charlie when he was Morgan's age, and he had the same thin curly blond hair and hazel eyes. Now he was bald and shorter than all of his sons. Still, he looked like he could take them in any fight, a fact the brothers liked to brag about.

He'd brought me a four-foot-tall stuffed Statue of Liberty. I pretended to think it was way cool, but I didn't know what I was supposed to do with it. Charlie didn't seem to know, either. He said, "I thought you'd find it ironic, Bug." Bug is his pet name for me. My dad thinks I'm both younger and older than I really am.

Charlie took the brothers and me to a fancy sushi place downtown for dinner. I ate a plate full of California rolls and drank two bottles of Orangina. He asked Morgan about his "course work" and Quills, whom he called by his real name, Michael, about the "prospect of his rock band" making it big, and wondered if Mark Clark had any advice about a computer problem some lady in their New York office was having. We could tell by the way he talked about the lady that she was his new girlfriend.

On Wednesday, he left again, this time for Los Angeles.

I checked MontgomeryHighChat.com every night, but there were no more new posts about Jordan.

On Thursday after school, I'd gone home and found a dark blue jeans skirt at the bottom of my closet. I wore that and a red long-sleeved T-shirt, plus some clunky black Doc Martens. I put on some mascara and lip gloss. I found a baby-blue corduroy book bag that I'd forgotten I owned, a Christmas present from someone. I pinned a few buttons on it—a Green Day button I had from the concert I went to with Quills, and one I found in a glass dish in a corner of the messy desk that said YOU'RE WEIRD. I LIKE THAT. I was sure I could pass for a ninth grader.

I showed up at Montgomery High at around two o'clock, at the beginning of seventh period. Montgomery High School is a big public high school, built of red brick, with white pillars in the front. Every once in a while Hollywood uses it for a movie.

It had been drizzling all day. The halls of Montgomery High were wide and smelled like cafeteria food, floor wax, and wet hair. They were mostly empty.

I'd found a manila envelope in the third-floor study at home and wrote PANSY BURROWS on the front with black Magic Marker. On my way to the front office, I passed by classrooms, all with their doors closed, the muffled sound of lecturing from inside. One door had a sign over it: MR. TARKINGTON'S CHAMBER OF COMMAS. Ha ha.

I waited in the main office for about a year and a half before a lady with long folksingerish hair and a purple woven shirt appeared from another office in the back and asked me if she could help me.

"Mr. Tarkington needs this delivered to Pansy Burrows," I said.

The lady put her hand out to take it.

"Uh," I said. I'd been doing pretty well pretending I was a ninth grader at Montgomery High. It hadn't occurred to me that the school secretary would volunteer to deliver the empty envelope for me. "Mr. Tarkington said I should take it straight to her classroom. I don't know where she is, though. Pansy Burrows, what class she's in right now. So I can deliver this. To her."

I wondered when, if ever, my mouth would close and words would stop coming out.

The secretary looked hard at my eyes, probably trying

to see if I was on drugs or something. I smiled back at her, hoping I didn't have any grilled cheese sandwich left in my braces from lunch.

She sat down at her desk and typed at her computer for a minute.

"Pansy Burrows . . . seventh period . . . Mrs. Yeoman's class."

I held my breath. Did she think I knew where Mrs. Yeoman's classroom was? "I'm only a freshman," I said. "I don't know where that is."

"Room 203," she said.

I thanked her. You could tell she smelled something fishy.

There was half an hour left before school let out. I found room 203 on the second floor, at the end of the hall across from the girls' restroom. I sat in a stall, the empty envelope between my knees, waiting for the bell to ring. One of the faucets dripped in the sink. Two girls came in, used the mirrors, and left. What if Pansy wasn't in school today? Or what if when the students spilled out of room 203, I lost sight of her in the crowd? Pansy was short. But she had that red hair . . .

The bell blared overhead. I jumped so high I banged my elbow on the metal toilet paper dispenser.

I rushed out of the bathroom just in time to see the back of Pansy's head moving off down the hall. She was talking loudly to friends on either side, making circles with her arms and ducking her head, acting out some drama, probably. I stayed as far behind her as I dared, following her out of Montgomery High and into the gray, drizzling afternoon.

- 13 -

PANSY BURROWS WAS POSSIBLY THE SHORTEST senior at Montgomery High. Lucky, for me, her hair was a beacon, a perky orange-red splotch among all the taller brunettes and dark blondes. Pansy Burrows walked fast, and the halls were packed with students. Half of the girls were dressed in shorts, tank tops, and flip-flops, as if the day were sunny and hot instead of chilly with drizzle. The halls smelled like wet clothes and too many different kinds of fruity perfumes. The students surged toward the doors. I got pushed back against the lockers and was bounced against a girl fixing her messy bun in the tiny mirror hung inside her locker. I muttered, "Sorry," and she released a small smile at me before slamming the locker shut. "No worries," she said.

For some reason, that made my heart feel big in my chest, that little meaningless smile, that "No worries."

I looked like I belonged there. I did not look like some freak show loser. I did not look like a seventh grader even.

But in that one minute I paused just to feel happy, I lost Pansy Burrows.

I saw her red hair bobbing along the wide sidewalk outside. I pushed down the stairs and out the doors. She was striding down the sidewalk with a tall, dark-haired chum on either side of her. She didn't seem like a cling-on with these girls; they looked like real friends. They had their arms interlocked and were skipping/walking in some goofy way that was part of some private joke, probably, or out of a movie. Whatever it was, it put them a good block ahead of me.

They turned right on Broadway, and I thought they must be going to catch the bus. There was a stop near the corner. A couple of old guys snoozed on the bench, and a gang of students tried to squeeze beneath the glass roof.

I wasn't sure what to do if Pansy stopped and waited for the bus. Stand and wait with her? I'd been so pleased with myself for figuring out a way to find her, I'd sort of forgotten that I was going to have to talk to her.

I went over my theory again in my head, that Pansy had literally stolen Jordan's identity as the ultimate cling-on move, as a way of *becoming* Jordan. You saw this sort of thing in a lot of psycho killer movies. I was still working on how this related to Dwight's murder, but it was awfully suspicious that Pansy Burrows was hanging out all nervouslike in Under the Covers the day before Dwight was murdered.

I chewed on my thumb cuticle. For a second I wished I had Jupiter with me. Reaching inside my pouch and stroking his fur always calmed me down. I told this to Reggie once. He told me a rabbit's foot would serve the same purpose. I'd had to pinch his arm for that one.

Pansy's two chums peeled off at the bus stop, but Pansy kept walking, head down, hands in her pocket. She swung a little as she walked, probably listening to music, an iPod or a CD player in the woven bag slung over her shoulder.

The drizzle stopped and the sun leaped out suddenly, blinding me. I kept on going, past the bus stop, on down Broadway. I had no clue where Pansy was off to. Broadway was lined with shops, small businesses, and about eighty-seven Starbucks; no one lived on Broadway.

I stayed a block behind her. It was easy. She never

looked up or turned around. It made me wonder why, in movies, when people tail other people, they were always ducking into doorways or stopping to pretend to window-shop. It's completely unnecessary.

As we cruised along, I tried not to think about the pile of dishes waiting for me at home and who might be around to see that I wasn't doing them. Mark Clark—still at work. Quills? Work. Morgan? Studying for finals, hopefully. I didn't want to think what would happen if I started slacking off dish duty and not showing up when I was supposed to. I've never been in that much trouble before.

At Broadway and 18th I spied Under the Covers down two blocks, on the other side of the street, and suddenly I knew Pansy Burrows was headed to the bookstore, where we first met. Just as this occurred to me, she stopped at the corner, waiting for the light to change. Pansy fussed with her CD player, hidden in her shoulder bag. She frowned, tapped her tiny foot. She looked so *overdone*, with her Curious George baseball shirt, jeans miniskirt, black fishnets, tie-dyed high tops, and pigtails. Long dangling earrings. Rings on most of her fingers. It was the too much of someone who was trying to make up for being too little. I felt sorry for Pansy Burrows.

Sure enough, Pansy skittered across the street and

ducked into Under the Covers. I was breathless with guessing right, and also with the thought of returning to the scene of Dwight's murder. The crime scene tape was gone by now. On *Law & Order* it always seemed to be up for weeks.

Inside the shop I half expected to see Dwight behind the counter, but of course it was someone else, a woman with short blond hair and those half glasses old people always wear, except this lady wasn't that old. She wore bracelets that jingled when she moved. She was flipping through a stack of papers. She smiled at me without really seeing me and went back to her work.

I could feel my heart pounding in my ears. I kept imagining Dwight's body lying on the floor behind the counter. The store had wood floors. Does blood stain wood?

I made myself focus. I could not afford to freak out.

Pansy stood at the magazine rack, her back to me. I had no clue what to do. Out of the corner of my eye, something drew my attention: the plastic tub of glittery sea-blue eyeglass cases. I sidled over and picked through the cases, buying time. I opened one and snapped it closed too quickly, and Pansy turned around. She looked right at me, then went back to her magazine.

I picked up a copy of *Teen Vogue* and flipped through

it. When she looked up at me again, I said, "Pansy Burrows. Remember me? Minerva Clark?"

"Oh sure. How you doing?" she said, closing her magazine around her pointer finger.

I could tell she still hadn't figured out who I was.

"I'm Jordan Parrish's cousin. We met here last week."

"Oh *right*! How are you? How's Jordan? I used to see her here, like, every day about this time. Haven't seen her since last week, though. She okay?"

This was my chance. "Uh, no, she's not okay. How could she possibly be okay?"

Pansy played dumb. "I saw her at lunch yesterday. She looked fine to me."

I felt myself coming down with a bad case of impatience, like a flu bug that crashed in out of nowhere.

"She's pretty together. Even after someone framed her by giving the cops her name when she was arrested. Did you know that little stunt may cost her the Hightower Scholarship? And if she doesn't get the Hightower she won't be able to go to college?"

"I heard it might be going to someone else, yeah." She glanced down for the briefest moment.

"Well, QT_PIE865, of course you know. You posted it in your flame. Why Jordan, Pansy? What's she ever done to you?"

"You're on crack," she said, slamming the magazine back on the rack and turning on her heel. The magazine slid to the floor. The lady behind the counter looked up. I smiled too big, knelt in a ladylike fashion to fetch the magazine and replace it properly, then followed Pansy out of the store.

"I'm really just trying to find out who did this to Jordan and why," I called after her as she marched down the street.

"Why do you care?" she spat back at me. "Don't you have anything better to do? Aren't you, like, in sixth grade or something? Aren't you supposed to be home listening to Avril Lavigne and playing with plastic horses?"

"Why do you care if I care?" I said, catching up with her in about five steps. "That flame came from your computer."

"I don't know what you're talking about," she nearly shouted. Her face was the color of the summer's first sunburn.

"The IP address of the computer is registered to your dad."

She folded her arms and kicked at something nonexistent on the sidewalk. "Zoe did it. I was downstairs getting chewed out by my mom for forgetting to take out the recycling or something and Zoe got on my computer."

I didn't know what she was talking about. Then I remembered Julia mentioning to me that Zoe McBride, another girl at Montgomery High, was the next in line for the scholarship if they wound up pulling it from Jordan. I didn't know anything about Zoe and I didn't understand why she would flame Jordan.

"There's a lot of gossip and stuff at school about how Zoe so totally does not deserve the Hightower. Not just that, but Zoe's family is pretty rich. She'd get to go to college anyway. People feel really sorry for Jordan. It's all, 'poor Jordan this and poor Jordan that.' Zoe just wanted everyone to know that Jordan isn't the perfect princess everyone thinks she is."

I bit my lip, less painful than biting your tongue, and it accomplishes the same thing. The taste of my strawberry-kiwi lip gloss distracted me for a minute. I wanted to shout like a big baby, "Don't say that about my cousin!" but that didn't seem the right thing to do. Something in Pansy's round, freckled face said she was telling the truth.

"I'm not saying that what Zoe did was cool, flaming her like that . . ." Her voice trailed off. She folded her arms across her chest. I tried to recall the exact words of the flame, something about Jordan being a poseur, something about how it was time people finally got wise to her. I thought about how she lied to me about being with Toc on Valentine's Day. Then a thought dropped into my head from nowhere: I remembered how when my mom and dad got divorced my mom tucked my hair behind my ear and said, "Sometimes even people you think you know backwards and forwards can surprise you." I didn't have a clue then what this meant. Now I was starting to get it.

"What do you mean about Jordan not being a perfect princess?" I asked.

"I'm not totally sure," she said, fumbling in her bag, then pulling out a pack of cigarettes.

"You smoke?" I said. *D'oh.*

"Remember when I saw you guys here whenever that was, last week? And she was like, 'Pansy Burrows, how are you?' like I didn't see her here *every* afternoon at the same time?"

"Not really, but go on." I remembered something like that, a weird skip in the conversation.

She lit her cigarette, then inhaled and exhaled quickly. "My mom works at that dry cleaners on the corner, and every day after school I come and hang out here until she gets off work. Every day. And Jordan's always here. And I mean always. She comes in, she talks to Dwight, or talked to Dwight I guess. Sometimes he'd give her one of those cases—the ones on the counter by the cash registers?—and she'd tuck it in her backpack. She never looked inside, never took out any sunglasses or anything, never bought a book, never stayed longer than about five minutes."

I could see Pansy was getting amped about this. She'd thought about it a lot, too. I guess that's what comes of being a reporter for the high school newspaper.

"I don't see how that makes her a bad person."

"No one said she was a bad person. She's just not Miss Perfect. She's into something. Maybe selling pot or something. I don't know what, and I don't think Zoe knows anything, but the point is that if someone is out to get Jordan or whatever, she's probably got it coming, and it's probably someone who isn't like your average high school student or whatever. That's just my opinion."

The sky was now a sad, flat gray, more like February than May. I brushed a few drops of rain from my cheeks and nose. "That is weird." I couldn't think of anything else to say. Suddenly, I felt so tired. I hadn't taken a nap since I was a little kid, but I could have used one then.

Pansy stared up at me, blew a smoke ring. "Why *do* you care? I mean, it's not like it's any business of yours."

"I don't know," I said. "Jordan used to be my idol. We were in *The Sound of Music* together once."

Pansy narrowed her eyes. "Oh wow. It was our spring

play a couple of years ago. You were one of the von Trapp children."

"Louisa," I said. "The one who sobbed all the time."

"I was on the tech crew," said Pansy.

"Really? Cool," I said.

"So you're just trying to get to the bottom of this because . . ."

"It bugs me how no one seems to care. There's the stuff with Jordan, but also the fact that the cops arrested the wrong person for Dwight's murder, some poor homeless dude who really had nothing to do with it."

"You're curious," said Pansy. "You've got the mind of an investigative reporter, just like me."

"They think because I'm thirteen I can't possibly find anything else interesting except myself."

Pansy laughed, wished me well, and hurried into the dry cleaners at the corner. I heard the electronic bell chime from where I stood on the sidewalk in the rain.

Back at Casa Clark no one was home. Normally, I like someone to be there when I come home, but that afternoon I was happy to be alone. The dirty dishes were stacked high in both sinks, glass and china towers carefully balanced by my evil brothers. The counters were covered with glasses. Most of them had only had water in them, I knew. There was not one clean fork or spoon left in the silverware drawer. I sighed. As long as I was madly scrubbing when someone walked in the door I'd be cool.

I fetched Jupiter out of his cage and did some ferret surfing, where I dragged him around on a dish towel and he stood in the middle with his nose up, his short legs apart for balance, big kahuna. We ran around and around the sofa until I nailed my shin on the corner of the coffee table. That hurt.

On the floor next to the front door a pile of mail lay beneath the mail slot. I limped over to see if maybe there was something for me. I used to have a subscription to *American Girl*, which is so lame and which I would never ever read, but still, I missed having something come for me.

So I was surprised to see a long white envelope addressed to me. Someone had printed my name and address off a computer and taped it to the envelope, no return address.

Inside there was a sheet of white paper that said:

Me quit
I'M you

I held the paper between both hands, which had started trembling. I stared at the rebus—Quit following me, I'm bigger than you—and then I stared at my hands.

I was truly amazed. I'd thought "trembling with fear" was just an expression.

There was a small crash, a scrabbling sound. I jumped about ten feet and dropped the letter. Seventeen million questions hopped around in my head all at once, like kernels of popping corn.

What was that noise? What had I done to deserve a death threat? Because that's what this was. Someone telling me to stop following them or else? But who? Who would send a death threat to a seventh grader? Jordan? Toc? The identity stealer of Jordan? The murderer of Dwight? Was it only a joke perpetrated by Reggie? Or even Hannah or Julia? What *was* that noise?

Only Jupiter, bored because we'd stopped ferret surfing before he was ready. He'd knocked my baby-blue corduroy book bag off the coffee table, where I'd left it. The flap had opened when it hit the floor, and the dang creature was crawling around inside. Jupiter loved nothing more than getting into a bag full of stuff. I felt a twitch of longing for the girl I was only a few weeks before, who loved nothing more than playing with her ferret.

I wanted Mark Clark to come home. I wanted Quills and Morgan to come home. I wanted them to come home so I wouldn't be alone, but I did not want them to come home and find this rebus. If they knew I'd received a death threat, they wouldn't let me out of their sight, much less out of the house.

And death threat rebus or no death threat rebus, there were a few things I still needed to do.

- 14 -

THE HIGHTOWER SCHOLARSHIP OFFICE ADDRESS was right on their Web site. It was easy enough to get there after school on Friday. Morgan didn't have any classes on Friday, so he was the BIC that day; I found him in the garage fussing around with the front wheel of his mountain bike. I told him I was going to the library to work on a report, and he said, "Great." Then he heaved the bike up by its handlebars and gave the wheel a big spin. I felt deeply bad that I was getting so good at telling white lies, but I told myself this was the last time. Morgan didn't even tell me to be careful crossing the street. Sometimes I don't think Morgan is qualified to be the BIC, but whatever.

I made Reggie go with me. I was too freaked out by

my death threat rebus to go by myself. During the bus ride I filled him in on the new information I'd gleaned from Pansy Burrows, that it looked as if Jordan and Dwight might be in on the checking account number scheme together. Or anyway, Jordan knew more than we thought she did, and that she was maybe not even an eighty percent good person, maybe more like sixty-six percent.

"I'm thinking maybe she didn't even save up for her car. Or, she did save up, but it wasn't, like, from a job or anything. It was stolen money." I told him about her necklace, the small gold J filled with diamonds.

"This is so *awesome*," said Reggie. He ripped open a pack of Shock Tarts with his teeth and dumped about half in his mouth. Reggie brought his skateboard with him everywhere he went, and he had it slung across his lap like a TV tray table. "I can't believe your cousin is a real crook."

"Well, we're not totally sure. But we're kind of giving up trying to solve the mystery. That's why we're going to the Hightower office."

I sighed and looked out the window. A mom jogging with a baby stroller huffed past us. I hated to say that the death threat rebus scared me enough to stop snooping around, but it had. I knew I was supposed to think, "No one will ever scare me away from finding out the truth!"

like all the one hundred percent good sleuths did, but I really did want to make it to my eighth-grade graduation. I'd also reached a dead end. If it wasn't Toc, and it wasn't Pansy Burrows, I had no clue who it was. It was someone I didn't know and couldn't seem to get to, either.

I'd tried to call the Hightower office, but no one ever answered. If I could set the record straight maybe then Jordan's problems would be all her own, and I could go back to minding my own business, and not be a Nosy Parker. I would do a super fine job on my Boston Tea Party report. I would get through the rest of the school year without talking to Hannah, who was turning out to be meaner than Cruella Deville. I would pay more attention to Jupiter. I would take Junior Lifeguard over the summer, and maybe learn to play the guitar.

But for now, all I wanted was the people who gave out the Hightower to know once and for all that Jordan deserved the scholarship. I could tell them what happened the day she was pulled over. Part of me also knew that I didn't want to find out any more bad things she might be into. No matter what else she'd done, she had had her identity stolen, she'd been framed—

"Wait a minute. Wait a minute. Wait a minute!" I said, sitting up straight. A few people looked up from their paperbacks.

"Jordan may be a crook, but she was still framed. The cop pulled her over for a smashed taillight, but when she picked me up—remember, I was walking home from Tilt—the light wasn't broken. It was totally fine. I remember, because I'd had a chance to read her bumper sticker, 'Blond if you're Honk.'"

"She's not one of those chicks who parallel parks by feel, is she? 'Cause she could have smashed the light then," said Reggie, flipping back his bangs.

"I didn't hear anything."

"So that means someone broke it when you guys were in the bookstore," said Reggie.

"Maybe Clyde the homeless guy?" I said.

"Or the person who stole her identity, who knew she'd eventually be pulled over for a broken taillight."

I wondered. Suddenly, I felt the urge to be back on the case. Reggie reached up and pulled the cord to signal our stop.

The Hightower was such a big deal in our state, I expected the office to be a big-deal office, but it was on the top floor of an old green house just off NW 23rd Avenue. We stood outside on the sidewalk, double-checked the address. On the first floor was a nail salon. Through the huge, clean window I could see ladies perched at little tables, getting their fingernails painted.

There was a light on in the second-floor window. A

wooden staircase hugged the side of the house, leading up to the second floor. We stood there for a few long minutes. I cracked my knuckles.

"I think I should go in by myself," I said.

"'S cool," said Reggie. I couldn't tell whether he minded or not. He kicked his skateboard from where it'd been resting on his thigh and rolled off down the sidewalk.

"Come back in fifteen minutes!" I shouted after him.

The office was one big room with a lady sitting at a desk and a smaller room behind her. There was a big pinky-beige flowered sofa against one wall, very girly, and black-and-white pictures of women from long ago hanging on one pinky-beige wall. Some of the women wore graduation gowns.

The lady had thick dark, shoulder-length hair and a long nose. Down-turned hazel eyes that looked kind and sad at the same time. I was so surprised that she didn't look like crabby Sister Patrice at school—what I always imagined all ladies in charge of things looked like—that I blurted out, "Are you the one in charge around here?"

She laughed, took off her glasses, looked me up and down. I hadn't bothered changing out of my uniform. It was just me, Minerva Clark, in my blue Holy Family T-shirt, khakis, and tennis shoes, my mess of a head of hair hanging down on either side of my head. "That depends on what you mean by in charge," she said. "Have a seat. What can I do for you?"

"I have some information about Jordan Parrish, just, you know, I thought someone should know. Someone in charge of things. She still deserves the Hightower." Even as these words came out of my mouth, I wondered if she *did* deserve it. I didn't want to think about that now. I just wanted to do what I'd come to do.

"Oh yes," she said. She folded her hands over her papers. "I'm Emma Larson, by the way."

"Minerva Clark. Jordan's my cousin."

"Ah," said Emma Larson. Like Mark Clark, she was the kind of serious responsible person who could only be called by two names.

I sat on the edge of the girly couch. I rubbed my sweaty palms on my thighs. I had that same old feeling of having a really good idea at home in my bedroom, then realizing how lame it was only after it was too late. And now my mind felt all mixed up by this new realization about Jordan's smashed taillight.

Emma Larson sat. She waited. From the other room came a strange noise, like someone was whispering.

Crap.

"I just wanted to say that I was with Jordan that day she was arrested and that it turned out to be a mistake.

You can even ask my dad. He's a lawyer. I mean, no matter what your criminal background check thingy said, she didn't do anything. She was pulled over for a broken taillight and then it turned out that someone had stolen her identity and—"

"Criminal background check thingy? What do you mean?" asked Emma Larson.

"You know, the final double-check before you give her the money."

Emma Larson now was looking at me like I was mad. The weird whispering noise coming from the other room was getting louder. Actually, it was less like whispering than like someone going, "Pssst!"

"Last week . . ." Her voice trailed off as she flipped through a black date book. "We received a phone call actually . . . on Thursday, the nineteenth, it looks like . . . It was left with the message service after hours, around six o'clock. A friend of the foundation calling to let us know that Ms. Parrish had been arrested."

Thursday the nineteenth? That was the day this whole mess had begun.

The hissing was getting louder and louder. Suddenly, it tipped over into a high scream. A teakettle. The smaller room must be a kitchen. "Do you want some tea?" asked Emma Larson, standing up and going to the kitchen.

"Sure," I said. I hated tea. Grown-up tea tasted no different than the "tea" Reggie and I used to make out of sticks and leaves in preschool.

All I could think was *Someone called, someone called, someone called.* I couldn't remember who said it was a criminal background check—I wasn't even sure what that was, quite frankly, but the point was, there was no background check. It was a phone call.

Someone deliberately ratted Jordan out. Probably the person who broke her taillight and who gave the cops her name in the first place, the same person who murdered Dwight in broad daylight.

I hopped up from the girly couch and whipped around the side of Emma Larson's desk.

"Would you like peppermint?" she called from the other room. "I know when I first began drinking tea that's what I liked."

"Sounds great," I called, too loudly. I read the entry in the black book, but there was no name, no number.

"Or apple-cinnamon?"

"Uh-huh!" I caught sight of the phone; it was just like the one we had at Casa Clark, with the built-in Caller ID. Beneath the screen was a little button labeled CID; hit that and you could scroll back until the dawn of time, to see who called and when.

"So which is it?"

I pressed the button about seven thousand times until I got back to the nineteenth. There were six numbers: Hurd Alan C. Out of Area. An unknown caller had called three times.

Then the jolt of a name I recognized:

Hollingsworth Tiffani.

I grabbed a pen from a mug on the corner of the desk and scribbled the number on my palm. I scampered back to the girly couch just in time for Emma Larson to bring back my cup of boiling water flavored with dirt and sticks. The white mug said A WOMAN'S PLACE IS IN THE HOUSE—AND THE SENATE.

I thanked her, put my lips to the rim, could tell it was scalding, took a sip anyway. "Auh!" I said.

"Be careful," she said. "Hot."

What would we talk about now? What was I doing here? Emma Larson looked at me, expecting me to go on. All I wanted to do was get out of there and call the Tiffani Hollingsworth number. It was probably her cell. I tried not to want this. I tried to remember that the whole reason I'd come to the Hightower Scholarship office was to tell someone what I knew so that I wouldn't have to think about it anymore, sort of like taking a lost dog to the pound. I wanted to drop off this half-solved mystery with Emma Larson and let her feed and water it and worry about it. Instead, I was back to obsessing.

"In any case," said Emma Larson, settling herself back in her chair, "we're still following up on the tip. Nothing's been decided. Your cousin just needs to sit tight for the time being."

I blew on my tea. Why did people drink this stuff? "Well, I just thought you should know."

"I'll be sure to look into it," said Emma Larson. I could tell she never would. "Your cousin is lucky to have someone so concerned about her well-being."

"Yeah, well. I'm a freak," I said. I could never drink this whole thing. In the movies, people always made a big production about serving people something to drink, then no one ever finishes drinking whatever it is. Have you noticed? Reggie told me this was stage business, something the actors did with their hands so they weren't just standing there like meatheads delivering their lines. But Emma Larson had the kettle on before I came in, so it couldn't have been stage business. Suddenly, I felt as if my brain was going to explode and spew out of my ears. Tiffani Hollingsworth? *Tiffani Hollingsworth?* Could it really be what it looked like? Jordan said the first person she'd called after the police had hauled her off to jail was Tiffani. Did Tiffani then turn around and call here?

"Thanks for the tea." I slid the mug onto the edge of the cluttered desk, and walked out before Emma Larson had a chance to speak. Lucky the office was so small; I was out the door and down the steps in a heartbeat.

The minute I hit the sidewalk I pulled my Emergencies Only cell phone out and punched in the number on my hand. It was already starting to smear from the sweat. Maybe the rat was another Tiffani Hollingsworth. That wasn't such an uncommon name, was it?

I didn't expect the person on the other end of the number to pick up on the first ring.

Yes, it was her. My old best babysitter, my cousin Jordan's best friend.

"Hi, Tiff, I was wondering if . . . I wanted to talk to you about what's going on with Jordan and why she was so mad at me the other day when I saw you guys after Rose Princess practice. I mean ambassador. You know what I mean."

"Who is this?" she asked.

"Oh! It's Minerva Clark."

She laughed. "You don't always need to say your last name, Min. I don't know any other Minervas."

I laughed, too. I was out of breath from walking so fast. A woman talking on her own cell phone while pushing an enormous baby carriage looked at me hard as we passed each other on the sidewalk.

It felt good to be laughing with Tiffani. Maybe there

was another reason she called Emma Larson and the Hightower people. Maybe she wanted to warn them that when they actually did do their criminal background check thingy, they should ignore it because it was a mistake.

"Where are you?" she asked.

"Where am I?" Why didn't I want to tell her where I was? It was a simple question.

"At the library, researching a paper."

"Wow, you still have papers due this late in the school year? Middle school must have gotten a lot harder."

"Yeah, it's on the Boston Tea Party." Liar! You are not at the library. You are not researching a paper. And you haven't even started the Boston Tea Party report.

Crap! I'd forgotten to wait for Reggie. I spun back around and retraced my steps back down 23rd. I walked faster and faster. I almost tripped over one of those little green metal tables that sit outside coffee places in this part of town.

"Why don't you stop by here? I'll be taking lunch in half an hour."

Lunch? It was four thirty. What was she talking about? Why was I suddenly so wigged out? I pulled a piece of hair out from behind my ear and starting tugging on it. Ack! I was turning into Quills, with his mad hair tugging. I stopped, retraced my steps, and sat at the green metal table I'd nearly tripped over. I tried to catch my breath.

"Isn't it late for lunch?" I asked.

Tiffani laughed again. She was a much bigger laugher than Jordan, who was a more serious girl altogether. "I'm working at Nordstrom now. In the mall. Meet me at the food court, at Panda Panda, in half an hour. I'll buy you an egg roll."

I said okay. I had used the Emergency Only phone for a nonemergency. I had lied to Morgan about my where-abouts. I had stalked off without waiting for Reggie, whom I'd dragged across town with me. I had dishes at home, piles and piles of them. I was so busted. I was so dead. Still, I said okay.

- 15 -

AFTER I HUNG UP I WENT to the nearest Starbucks to ask for directions to the mall. It wasn't that far, but it was over one of the bridges that connects the two halves of our city. One barista dude asked another, who asked another. Eventually one of them told me what bus to take. Within twenty minutes I was standing in front of Panda Panda, cracking my knuckles and wondering whether this was what it was like to go insane.

The food court was packed with teenagers, mostly couples where the girls looked all hot and done up in their low-rise slacks and high-heel shoes, makeup perfect, hair perfect, and the boys looked like they just came from doing yard work. All the food court smells swirled together—french fries, melted cheese, spicy Chinese, chocolate chip cookies. Ugh. I felt sick.

Tiffani showed up just as I was thinking of calling Morgan or Quills and begging them to come get me. She was dressed up herself, which is part of working at Nordstrom. She wore a black skirt and blouse and a pair of really strange black suede platform clogs with a buckle and the thickest wooden sole ever. I stared at them as she clomped up to me.

"Aren't these cute?" she said, turning and lifting up her heel so I could admire them.

"Sure," I said. "Aren't they, uh, hard to walk in?"

"Not at all," she said, looking up at the menu over the counter. "They're totally comfy. I could get you a pair if you want. They'd be awesome on you."

"They'd make me about eight feet tall," I said. Why were we talking about these stupid clogs?

"Tall *rocks*, though. I wish I was taller. Five-ten at least. You and Jordan are lucky being tall. I'm just a little shrimp. It sucks. So what are you eating?"

"Could I just have a Sprite? Please."

"Still so polite! Even when you were a little kid you always said 'peas.' Do you remember that? How you used to say 'peas' instead of 'please?'"

"I don't think that was me."

"Well, whatever!" she said gaily.

After she ordered we found a table and sat. "So you're looking hot these days. Is it just growing up, or what?"

"I don't know," I said. "I'm using a new shampoo."

Tiffani laughed and clapped her hands. "Yeah, that's it."

I said, "How is my cousin? I'm worried about her." This seemed as good a place as any to start. One of the things I was learning is that sometimes you just needed to start talking, and what you needed to say would come to you.

"I'm worried about her, too!" said Tiffani. "You know, she's gotten even thinner. I wish I could lose some weight. How do you think she does it? I don't think she's bulimic or anything. I mean, that's the kind of thing a best friend knows, you know?"

"Uh," I said. How on earth did we get talking about this? I had this strange feeling about Tiffani. She was so nice, but there was something else. It was the way you opened the refrigerator and smelled something going bad, but you couldn't find what it was.

The boy behind the counter at Panda Panda called out "Yo!" to Tiffani and waved her over to pick up her tray.

"Be right back!" she said.

But she wasn't right back. She stood and talked to him, shifting her weight from one foot to another, playing with her hair. She was about to take the tray, then it looked as if he'd forgotten the drinks, and there was another giggling exchange about that. He turned and took two cups from the stack near the soda machine.

I slouched in my seat. I bounced my leg. I waited.

Tiffani picked up the tray, tossed a giggle over her shoulder, and just as she started back to our table, turned around yet again. She'd forgotten the straws.

I sat up straight when I saw her coming and accidentally kicked her purse, which was sitting on the floor between us. It was a big leather bag that yawned open at the top.

Inside, winking up at me, was one of the glittery eyeglass cases from Under the Covers. I stared and stared at it. I was shocked to see it, but there was something else. It wasn't just any case, but the one that was more purple than blue, the one Jupiter had chewed the day Jordan and I had stopped at Under the Covers on the worst day of my life. All of a sudden I felt dizzy, like I'd just gotten off the Tea Cups at Disneyland.

"Sorry!" Tiffani sang out as she clomp-clomp-clomped back over to her seat across from me. "That guy is just such a hottie, don't you think? Or are you too young for that still?"

"That's a cool case," I said, looking down at her purse. I was sure she could hear my heart slamming around inside my chest.

"Wha—Oh that. Yeah, I love it. I get a lot of compliments on it."

"Is it for sunglasses, or what?"

Tiffani stopped, her plastic fork full of noodles dangling in midair. She looked at me as if she were trying to figure something out. She put her fork down, reached over, and pulled the glittery case from her purse. She turned it over, this way and that. "It is pretty cool, isn't it?"

"Where'd you get it?"

"You know, I can't remember. Maybe it was a present."

We both gazed at it like idiots. It was just a stupid eyeglass case. Of course, it wasn't just any eyeglass case. I could see a mangled spot on one end.

"What happened to it?"

"Where?"

"There." I pointed to the end, where it looked as if a puppy had gotten ahold of it.

A puppy.

Or as I knew, a ferret.

Pansy Burrows said Jordan came to Under the Covers every day, and every day Dwight passed Jordan a glittery eyeglass case. Dwight was obviously also passing eyeglass cases to Tiffani. But why? What was in the cases?

"You done admiring?" said Tiffani. One corner of her mouth crept up in a tiny smirk. She couldn't know I knew, because the truth of it was, I didn't know I knew. This was harder than any rebus I could ever think up.

"Yeah, I just got an idea for a new rebus. I've been writing a book of rebuses. Just for myself, you know."

I teased a napkin from under the edge of her paper plate, fished a pen out of my pocket, and wrote:

Clam storm

Tiffani turned the napkin around, chewed for a minute, then said, "The clam before the storm?"

She gave me a big fakey wink.

Oops! I scratched out "Clam" and wrote "Calm."

It *was* the calm before the storm, and I was sure it was Tiffani who'd sent me the death threat rebus. I was also sure that Tiffani had framed Jordan and killed Dwight. I just didn't know how. I hadn't thought about the part where I'd have to prove it.

It was close to six o'clock when I got home. The back door was locked, the garage door closed. I was glad it was nearly June, when it could be late and still not look late, when the sun lounged around in the western sky, as if it couldn't decide whether to set or just hang around for a few more hours. I prayed madly to the angel who watches over seventh-grade Nosy Parkers that no brothers would be home.

I closed the door quietly and then scooted straight to the kitchen to attack the piles of fake dirty dishes. Just as I reached the sink, I heard Mark Clark pull into the driveway. Thank you thank you thank you.

I turned on the hot water, squirted a small drop of lemon-fresh Joy into each one of the fake dirty drinking glasses lined up on the counter.

Behind me, I heard Mark Clark drop his keys on the counter. The warm water felt good on my hands. I was so relieved.

"What's new?" he asked.

"Notta lotta," I said.

"Say, I meant to ask, how'd your computer project turn out?" He took a glass out of the cupboard, poured himself about an inch of cranberry juice, then set the glass on the counter.

"What computer project?"

He poked me in the side. "The extra credit project I helped you with? Tracking the IP address?"

"Oh right! It was great. It really helped. With my grade. And everything."

He paused behind me but didn't say anything. He walked out. Then I heard the whirr of his computer booting up in the other room.

I didn't realize I'd been holding my breath.

*   *   *

Upstairs, I turned on my computer and logged on to MontgomeryHighChat.com. I didn't even try to see if Reggie was on. Even though he was my best friend, and even though he'd listened as I yattered on and on about the puzzle of who'd stolen Jordan's identity, something told me he wasn't the one who could help me put it all together. He didn't have the interest, for one thing, nor did he have a clue about how the minds of girls worked.

Ferretluver: If QT_PIE865 is around, could you send me an e-mail at Ferretluver@aol.com? It's super important.

Almost before I could even finish typing "important" an IM box popped onto my screen.

Grlreporter: Hi, Minerva Clark. What's the haps?

Ferretluver: Pansy? How did you know it was me?

Grlreporter: Just guessed. Don't know anyone else with a ferret. What's up?

Ferretluver: When you used to see Jordan at Under the Covers? Was Tiffani ever with her?

Grlreporter: Hollingsworth? Sometimes. Sometimes Tiffani would show up by herself.

Ferretluver: And would Dwight give her one of those eyeglass cases?

Grlreporter: Yup yup. That I saw anyway. Why?

I typed up a fierce storm of explanation. How I first thought Toc, who had a thing for Jordan, had stolen her identity to punish her for not loving him back. Then how I thought it was her, Pansy, because of the flame. I told her about my tea at the Hightower Scholarship office with Emma Larson, and my Sprite at the food court with Tiffani. I told her about Tiffani having the eyeglass case that my very own ferret had munched on that day at Under the Covers. I thought I'd typed everything I could think of. Then I remembered something.

Ferretluver: Toc told me that Dwight had a scheme going where he stole the checking account numbers of the little old ladies who bought books at Under the Covers. He would steal the numbers, order new checks using a different name—

Grlreporter: And then buy stuff for the next week or so, until the poor woman got her bank statement.

Ferretluver: How did you know?

Grlreporter: It happened to my aunt! Someone

printed checks on her account and spent about
$25,000.

Ferretluver: :-O

Grlreporter: I'm thinking Jordan and Tiffani
have something to do with it.

Ferretluver: Like they're all in it together???? It's
impossible!

Grlreporter: But what were they passing back
and forth in the glasses case? Did you get a peek
inside the one Tiffani has?

Ferretluver: No =(

Grlreporter: And there's also, like, the very real
possibility it wasn't the homeless man who killed
Dwight, but someone involved in this.

Ferretluver: He didn't! I figured it out. The
person who killed Dwight had to have been
right-handed, but Clyde Bishop had a with-
ered-up right hand. There's no way he could
have done it.

Grlreporter: I think it's time to tell some adult-
type person. Know any cops?

I thought of Detective Peech, with his tree trunk–sized
legs and stern gaze. He already thought I was a liar. I
couldn't imagine showing up at the police station with
this story. Even if Pansy came with me, we were still just

two girls obsessing over a pretty, more-purple-than blue eyeglass case. He'd think we were mad.

I stood up and paced around my room. Who? Who? Who? Mark Clark probably knew about computer identity theft and stuff, but I didn't think he'd know about stealing people's checking account numbers. Plus, I didn't want to risk him clicking into lecture mode about paying more attention to my schoolwork and less about some imaginary nefarious scheme involving murder.

I kicked at a pile of dirty clothes. Tomorrow was room cleaning day, and the space under my bed was already stuffed. I got depressed, all of a sudden, thinking how I'd have to do a real cleaning.

Then, I saw my extra long red Speedo swimsuit with the yellow flowers.

Grlreporter: You still there?
Ferretluver: Yep. And I know who can help us.

- 16 -

THAT MORNING I CLEANED MY ROOM as if getting
into heaven depended on it. I pulled everything out from
under my bed—dirty clothes, old assignments, pretty
boxes from old Christmas presents I insisted on keeping,
dried-up markers and Chap Stick tubes without their
caps—then swept. I dusted my bookshelves. Changed
my sheets. Cleaned my mirror with Windex. Everything.

I did every dish in the sink, on the counter, and
fetched every dirty glass and plate from Mark Clark's
computer room, the TV room, and even the basement.

Then I asked if I could go to the water park with
Pansy Burrows. I felt a little guilty, because normally I
would have asked Reggie, but Reggie was still a little

POed that I'd walked off without him the day before. Plus, I didn't want Reggie around if there was a chance I'd get to hang out with Kevin. This didn't make much sense to me, since Reggie was my friend and not, like, a boyfriend, but still.

Quills was the BIC that day. I found him outside with a friend from Kinko's. They stood in the driveway, their heads bent over the engine of the Electric Matador, talking automotive talk. The friend had an entire arm of green-and-blue tattoos.

Quills grilled me on my room and the dishes. "Did you pick up the dog poop in the backyard?" he asked.

"We don't have a dog," I said, rolling my eyes. This was an old joke, done for the benefit of the friend.

Pansy sped up a few minutes later in an old Ford Explorer. Fuzzy pink dice hung from the rearview mirror.

"Thanks for coming to get me," I said, sliding into the passenger seat.

"Do you know how to get there? I don't think I've ever been to the water park before. I'm so totally not a water park kind of person, know what I mean?"

Pansy wore a black-and-white print bucket hat jammed over her curly red hair and eye glitter on her lids. Some of it had gotten on her freckled cheeks. "Yeah, I can see that."

The instant we roared off down the street Pansy lit up a cigarette. I looked back through the rear windshield to see if Quills noticed. He didn't even look up from the engine. It was alarming to think the BIC would let me hop into a car with someone he'd never met.

"I so totally wouldn't be surprised if Jordan and Tiffani were part of some ring of thieves. Do you remember about five years ago, when Montgomery's student body president and his best friend robbed, like, about a dozen stores? They hit International Burrito there on Broadway, and what's the name of that bakery? And the Plaid Pantry. Guns, ski masks, the whole bit. They got arrested for armed robbery, and since they were eighteen, got tried as adults. Is Jordan eighteen?"

"I think so." I tried to remember. This was all starting to seem like a movie. My cousin Jordan a criminal? I realized that before, when I wondered whether she was a teen murderer, I didn't think it was really possible. I was just being a drama queen. I was just goofing with myself. This was like making up a rebus; it was a puzzle, a riddle. Part of me didn't believe my perfect cousin and now, my favorite former babysitter, could be involved in anything this illegal or uncool. Stealing money from poor old grannies. Come on! I had a feeling now that the part of me that didn't want to believe was going to be faced with a truth it couldn't deny. My armpits felt damp suddenly. I bounced my legs like a maniac.

I made myself feel better by remembering I was going to talk to Kevin. And it was for a real reason, not a fakey reason, which even boys can see straight through.

The water park was less crowded than usual, probably because the weather was warm and sunny, a real spring day, and parents were most likely telling their kids to go outside and play. It still smelled like chlorine and hot dogs, though. There was still a long line outside the equipment room, little kids in wet swimsuits waiting to rent inner tubes.

Kevin wasn't at the snack counter, and he wasn't at the main desk where you paid to go in, and he wasn't giving out inner tubes. Pansy and I bought drinks and sat on a bench across from the main desk.

"Are you sure the dude's working today?" asked Pansy. I detected some tone. Only I don't think it's tone when it comes from someone who's four years older.

"He works on Saturdays," I said. I didn't say, *Well, that one Saturday I met him.* "Maybe he's at lunch."

"Go ask somebody," said Pansy. She drained her drink, sucked the last drops through her straw, making that noise I was taught was impolite.

I didn't like that Pansy was ordering me around, but I

214

let it go. I stood up, wiped my palms on my jeans. Just as I reached the main desk, Kevin appeared, walking out from the men's locker room at the end of a long blue-and-green tiled hallway to the left of the desk.

He wore red swim trunks and a white T-shirt with the water park logo. His crunchy swimmer's hair was sticking out all over, the same way Quills's does when he has a hissy fit. My heart felt like it hiccupped when I looked into those mountain-lake blue eyes.

I was pretty sure he'd remember me, if only because he'd witnessed my maximum wedgie. I pushed that embarrassing thought out of my mind, or tried to. As he reached the main desk, I felt my face get hot. He said, "Hey" to the blond lifeguard-looking girl sitting there and chatted for a minute about his schedule.

"Kevin?" I asked. "I don't know if you remember me. I was—"

"Sure," he said, smiling. (Smiling!) "With the mean girlfriends." As he leaned past me to pick up a piece of paper off the desk I could smell his soap smell, his cinnamony breath. He was unlike most of the boys I knew, who always had some form of BO, or else they were wearing clothes that needed to be washed, or had just eaten some sour-cream-and-onion potato chips. Kevin was so clean. He didn't have zits. His nails weren't bitten or dirty.

"Anyway, I know this might strike you as totally lame, but I was wondering if I could talk to your mom."

He laughed a little, rolled up the schedule, and gave me a swat on the top of my head. "My mom? Why do you want to talk to her?"

"It's kind of a long story." I was tempted to fall back on the old lie and say I had a school assignment, but it didn't seem right. Too much was at stake, and anyway, Pansy knew the truth.

We strolled over towards where Pansy sat, legs crossed, madly text messaging someone. She glanced up at us from under the rim of her bucket hat, checked out Kevin but good, then leaped up, knocking her empty soda cup to the floor, causing the top to pop off and the ice to spill out.

"Ack!" Pansy shrieked. The same shriek as when Jupiter had jumped out of my book bag that day at Under the Covers and scampered along the counter. It occurred to me that Pansy was slightly overcaffeinated. She raced in an overly dramatic crouched-down run to the snack counter and yanked a wad of napkins from the dispenser, came back, and started scooping up the ice.

"It's okay. The carpet's waterproof," said Kevin.

She peeked up at him, and I knew at once that Pansy

thought Kevin was pretty dang hot. I'd hoped that she would do most of the talking, so I could spend most of the time sneaking peeks at Kevin, but curious Pansy, nosy Pansy, chatty Pansy had left the building, and in her place was a self-conscious girl who probably thought her legs were too short or her knees were too fat or her hair was too frizzy or you name it.

I could see it was going to be up to me. I sighed.

"Here's the thing," I began. "You told me your mom worked in the fraud division at the U.S. Bank or something, right?"

"Yup."

"My friend and I—"

"Pansy Burrows," said Pansy, dabbing at her wet fingers with the wet napkins, then sticking out her hand. She flashed her dimples. "You don't go to Montgomery, do you?" She *knew* he didn't go to Montgomery. I'd told her on the way over that I didn't know anything about him, really, other than that his mom would be able to help us.

Kevin looked down, played a little drum solo on his leg with the rolled-up schedule. "Uh, no. St. Thomas More."

"Isn't that a *middle school?*" asked Pansy.

A fizzy feeling of pure bubbly joy spun up through my insides. Kevin wasn't in high school at all! We played St.

Thomas More in basketball. It was a dorky K–8 Catholic school, just like Holy Family.

"We killed your girls in basketball this year," I said.

"Not the eighth graders," he said. "Our eighth-grade girls were undefeated."

"You're in eighth grade?" snorted Pansy. "Isn't that like, child abuse, making you have a job?"

"It's part of the lifeguard training program," said Kevin.

"Passing out inner tubes?" said Pansy, as if it was the lamest thing she'd ever heard.

Kevin shrugged.

We'd totally lost the thread of why we'd come all this way. The conversation felt like an eager dog at the end of one of those clothesline leashes. It had gotten away from us and was now twisted around a tree, sniffing somewhere under a shrub. And I wasn't particularly interested in getting the dog back. Kevin was in eighth grade! Practically my age!

Then he turned his head and looked towards the door. Did I mention his straight, perfect nose? "Well, here she is to pick me up. You can ask her yourself."

Ask who what? *Oh!* Right. Kevin's mom. The lady he introduced to us as Mrs. Snowden. Kevin Snowden. Minerva Clark-Snowden. That made me sound like a

British explorer. Or a tissue. Wasn't Clark-Snowden a toilet paper manufacturer? Get a grip, Minerva Clark. Get a grip.

Mrs. Snowden wasn't a young mom, but she was a cool mom. At Holy Family there were a lot of young moms, a lot of moms who'd had their first babies when they were, like, eighteen. Mrs. Snowden had some wrinkles, but she also had muscles in her arms. Her blondish hair was sort of crispy, too, just like her son's. She was probably a swimmer when she wasn't a high-powered executive ridding the world of bank fraud.

She bought herself a latte at the cart beside the snack bar and heard our story. She dabbed at the foam with the little red stirrer stick, but I could tell she was listening. I could tell she didn't think we were just stupid girls with overactive imaginations. I did most of the talking while Pansy kept patting her hair, which was getting frizzier by the moment.

We sat at a round table as far from the wave pool as possible, the better to hear each other. Kevin disappeared for a bit, then came back and sat down between me and Pansy.

"All right," said Mrs. Snowden, "let me make sure I have this straight. Someone was arrested last Valentine's Day and gave the police your cousin's name. You were trying to find out who this person was and stumbled upon the fact that a friend of your cousin—Dwight, is it?—was stealing the checking account numbers from the patrons of the bookstore where he works . . ."

"Right," I said. I hadn't told her that Dwight had been murdered yet. It sounded too extreme. I didn't want her to doubt us. I didn't want her to stop nodding her head and stirring her latte. I didn't want her to lose that thoughtful wrinkle between her dark eyebrows.

"And how does your cousin figure into this?" asked Mrs. Snowden.

"For the past couple of months I've seen Jordan—Minerva's cousin—at the bookstore every afternoon," said Pansy.

"Pansy goes there to wait for her mom, who works at the dry cleaners down the block," I added. I also didn't want Mrs. Snowden to have to work any harder at putting this together than necessary.

"And every afternoon, Dwight would pass Jordan an eyeglass case and she would put it in her knapsack. She never bought a book, and she never stayed long. It was like he was passing her a message. And the key thing is—" Pansy glanced at me, then cleared her throat a little—"it's well known that Jordan doesn't have a lot of money. Her mom has two jobs and Jordan's never had, like, cool clothes or a cell or a car or anything much.

Then, suddenly, after she started coming to the bookstore, she had, like, this awesome leather jacket and some really nice jewelry. She started getting her hair cut at some fancy salon downtown. She just had stuff. All of a sudden."

"And you said there was another girl involved? A friend."

"Her best friend, Tiffani Hollingsworth," I replied.

"Why do you think she's involved?"

"Because I saw the eyeglass case in her purse. Then she took it out and showed it to me. I also think, for some reason, that it was Tiffani who stole my cousin's identity, because right after Jordan was arrested, she called the Hightower Scholarship office and told them that Jordan—who won this year's grant—had been arrested. You're not allowed to have a record of any kind, I guess."

"So you think Tiffani was trying to get back at Jordan for . . .," asked Mrs. Snowden.

I looked at Pansy, who raised her eyebrows.

"We don't really know."

"And you don't know what was in these eyeglass cases everyone is apparently passing back and forth?"

"Well, I would feel really stupid if they were, uh, glasses," I said, trying for a joke.

Mrs. Snowden laughed. "I don't think we know quite

what's going on, but it doesn't sound as if we're talking about glasses here."

"There's one other thing," I said. "The guy at the bookstore, Dwight? He was murdered last week. The police arrested a homeless man who used to hang around outside . . ." My voice trailed off. Hearing me say it aloud to an adult was horrible. Talking about it with Reggie or Pansy was like talking about a movie. It was like talking about what if you found a bag in the street with a million dollars in it, or what if you found a skull buried in your backyard.

"Oh, that Dwight. I thought it sounded familiar," said Mrs. Snowden. "I remember reading about that in the paper."

I told her about Clyde's withered right hand and how Dwight had been hit on the left side of his head, and how, given that, Clyde would never have had the strength with his right hand to hit Dwight hard enough to kill him. "And I don't think I'm being a drama queen about this, but I think it may have been Tiffani who killed him."

Mrs. Snowden released a small smile then, and I knew we were doomed. I think the word is "patronizing." She said, "You two are quite the detectives, aren't you?"

"There are a lot of teenaged boy murderers," I said. "Why can't there be teenaged girl murderers?"

"Detective *and* feminist!" she said.

I didn't know what that was.

"All right. All right." Then Mrs. Snowden pulled a small black leather notebook and pen from her bag. "The name of the bookstore is Under the Covers?" She wrote it down. She had nice handwriting, not too round and loopy, but sharp and confident.

"It's on Northeast Broadway."

"I don't know what you girls have here. I'll see if there's any connection with customers from our bank who've been the victims of checking account fraud and this bookstore."

I exhaled, slumped back in my chair. I didn't realize I'd been holding my breath. How can you talk and not breathe at the same time? This was good. Now Mrs. Snowden would fix things. She'd be able to use all her high-powered bank executive techniques to connect Jordan and Tiffani and the glittery eyeglass cases to Jordan's identity theft and Dwight's murder. She'd find out why Tiffani had called the Hightower Scholarship office after Jordan had been arrested, and maybe, maybe she'd be able to come up with some evidence that Tiffani was guilty of Dwight's murder.

Then I could go back to being Minerva Clark. Although I doubted I would be going back to the same Minerva Clark I was before I was electrocuted, before I discovered that if you walked through the world thinking you were just fine the way you were, people would treat you that way.

I glanced over at Kevin, who'd made an origami box out of the schedule he'd been carrying around.

Mrs. Snowden closed her notebook. "I appreciate your telling me about this, ladies. It's good information to have."

Good information to have? That didn't sound as if she were going to fix things. I looked over at Pansy. She bugged her pale eyes out a little, making a "what are you going to do?" face.

"Aren't you going to call the police or something?"

For the first time Mrs. Snowden smiled in that way adults do when they find you amusing. "I don't think there's really enough here to involve the police, do you?"

"Is it because we don't know what they've been passing back and forth in the eyeglass case?" I asked. I could hear the pleading in my own voice. Kevin even looked up from his folding.

"For starters, yes." Then she turned to Kevin. "You ready, Kev?"

She stood up; then he stood up. As they walked towards the exit he turned around and gave me a dorky-cute salute.

I felt tears surge into my eyes. I hadn't cried in so long,

and I wouldn't cry now. I gave Kevin the dorky-cute salute right back.

It was pretty clear that Mrs. Snowden had found us . . . entertaining . . . but she wasn't going to fix anything. Now what?

- 17 -

AS PLANS GO, iT WASN'T a great one, but it was all I could think of.

The next afternoon, Sunday, I scooped up Jupiter from his hammock and popped him into the pocket of my hoodie. It was another sunny day, and I didn't need a sweatshirt, but Jupiter traveled best in that front pocket. It would be easy to let him go and tuck him back in.

All the brothers were home when I left for the mall. Morgan was in the third-floor study, slouched in the big red leather chair, drinking green tea and writing in a notebook. Quills was in the basement with the drummer from Humongous Bag of Cashews—one of the guys whose names I could never remember—trying to fix his amplifier. Mark Clark was playing EQ and talking to someone on the phone at the same time.

Here's something I learned: When all the brothers were home, each thought one of the other ones was the BIC. I made sure all the dishes were done, turned up Green Day loud but not too loud in my room, closed my door, walked downstairs and straight out of the house. I would be back before anyone knew I was gone.

I hopped on the 77 bus and was at the mall in ten minutes. I'd already called ahead and found out that Tiffani was working that day. Luckily it was in Brass Plum, the department I would shop in if I ever went shopping.

Brass Plum was crammed with round racks of T-shirts, blouses, and skirts. Piles of jeans and cotton sweaters sat folded on a row of tables beneath a television on which a music video I didn't recognize played. The same video played on a huge screen behind the counter. There were tall racks of sunglasses and smaller racks of earrings, trays of earrings, bracelets, all kinds of sparkly girl junk that Jupiter would have gone crazy for, if he weren't dozing in my pocket.

I was already sweating.

Tiffani was replacing dresses on a rack. She looked different—she'd restreaked her hair, or maybe it was the low pigtails she wore. She looked trendy-hippie in a white peasant blouse and pink-and-blue patchwork skirt. She was frowning, and when she looked up and saw me, her thin mouth deepened into a bigger frown before switching into a fakey nice smile that was almost a sneer.

"Look who's here," said Tiffani. She gave the dresses on the rack a big shove to make room for the ones she was returning. "Can I help you?"

"Just looking," I said.

"Anything in particular?" she said. "Here's something that would look totally adorable on you." She held up a hideous lavender mini made of some crinkling material, with a big ruffle around the hem. It was the type of dress S Cubed or one of the Chelseas would wear. So totally not Minerva Clark, and she knew it.

"Sure," I said, staring straight back at her. "I'll give it a try."

"This is a two. You probably don't wear a two," she said.

"Probably not," I said. "Have anything else totally hot and adorable?"

She stared hard at me. She couldn't figure out what I was doing there, I could tell, but she knew it couldn't be anything good.

Luckily, at that moment a tall, skinny girl with hip bones that looked straight out of some documentary on dinosaurs and the lowest low-rise pants imaginable tapped Tiffani on the arm and asked about a shirt in another size and color. Tiffani smirked at me and went in search of the shirt.

I moved towards the counter and picked up one of the stupid charm bracelets on a pink velvet tray near the cash register. They were silver, with hearts and crescent moon charms.

I felt Jupiter stirring in my pocket. I stood up on my tip toes and peeked over the counter. I was counting on the fact that Tiffani was still carrying the same purse and that she hadn't gotten the zipper fixed. Behind the counter were cubbies filled with boxes and bags and the white tissue paper for wrapping your purchases.

My heart thumped in my chest. It felt way too big and powerful for one seventh-grade girl's nervous body. I didn't see Tiffani's bag anywhere. Maybe there was a place for employees to keep their things somewhere else in the store. I started feeling as if I'd gotten all worked up over nothing, as if this was yet another idea that had seemed terrific in the middle of the night when I'd thought of it, but was bad-movie stupid in the light of day.

I moved over to the side of the counter and glimpsed Tiffani's bag yawning open. Lucky, lucky day. And there it was, as I'd hoped, the glittery eyeglass case, the gnawed-on one that was more purple than blue, winking against the black lining of the bag. The one that proved Tiffani had been to Under the Covers to see Dwight after Jordan and I had left that afternoon but before Dwight's body had been discovered the next morning.

Tiffani was still on the other side of the department, checking tags for the girl with the hip bones.

It was now or never.

In one motion I pulled Jupiter out of my pocket, leaned behind the counter, and dropped Jupiter inside Tiffani's purse. He's a good boy: He went straight for the case, hauled it up and out of the bag, and scampered back to me.

Here's where I made the mistake that seemed deadly at first but turned out to be good. In that way it was a lot like the worst day of my life, when I'd made an idiot of myself at Tilt, saw my favorite cousin get arrested, and was electrocuted in front of a bunch of people while having a fractal made out of my brain waves.

I should have just tucked Jupiter and the eyeglass case back in my pocket and left, but I couldn't help myself. What if after all this there *were* only glasses in the eyeglass case?

It took two hands to pry it open. Inside, folded up to fit, were three copies of something official looking . . . a form of some kind . . . At the top I read "Nordstrom Credit Card Application."

"Hey!" Tiffani yelled from the other side of Brass Plum.

I looked up so fast I thought I'd broken my own neck. Tiffani was staring right at me. She'd seen everything.

I started walking fast, weaving my way between the racks, the bass line of the music video pounding in my ears, trying to refold the credit card applications with one hand while holding the eyeglass case with the other, and keeping Jupiter, who was now awake and raring to play, inside my pocket with my elbows.

I fast walked out of the department, past children's shoes. I could hear Tiffani clomping after me in her suede platform clogs. I think I heard her say, "You won't get away with this," but she wasn't yelling too loud. She wasn't making a scene. We even fast walked past a security guard, who was flirting with another salesgirl.

I realized then that I could have stopped and just handed over the eyeglass case to the security guard. Clearly, it was what it looked like. Tiffani was stealing the information off of credit applications. But I just kept thinking about Mrs. Snowden and how she needed more information, and, okay, I admit it, how it would be a good excuse to see Kevin again. Plus, when someone's chasing you, even at a fast walk, all you think about is getting away.

I plunged into the mall and started jogging. Jupiter

was going nuts. Snatching the eyeglass case had been tons of fun for him. I had to keep both sides of my hoodie's pocket closed, but that required both hands. I tried to slip the eyeglass case into my pocket but there wasn't enough room. Why hadn't I brought a book bag?

I jogged past Pacific Sunwear and Hot Topic. An African-American girl with a headful of beaded braids gasped and grabbed her friend's chubby brown arm: "I swear that girl had a rat in her pocket."

The mall was loud. Music blared from inside each shop, and Pumbaa's theme from *The Lion King* blared from the ice-skating rink at the mall's center.

I thought I'd lost Tiffani. I turned to look while at the same moment jogging past a vendor who sold glass wind chimes. Jupiter poked his head out, took one look at the wind chimes, and sprang from my pocket. I grabbed at him, but he squirted out of my hand like toothpaste. Hanging beneath the wind chimes were rows of glass animals, delicate horses and giraffes, elephants and fish. I lunged after Jupiter and cleared the shelf of glass animals. They made a high tinkling sound as they shattered on the floor. The vendor, an Indian man smaller than me, started shouting.

Then I saw Tiffani clomping after me, probably swearing, fists clenched.

I spied a plain beige door and lunged for it, hoping it

would eventually lead outside. The door slammed behind me. A long hallway extended in either direction. It smelled like new clothes, perfume, and stale fried food, the regular mall smell, only stronger. I didn't know which way to go, but it didn't matter. I took two steps in one direction before the door from the mall swung open.

It was Tiffani, only somehow she'd gotten shorter. She bared her teeth, called me a name seventh graders aren't supposed to say. She held one of her platform clogs above her, and before I could make a sound, she brought it down on my head. My final thought before I fell was not to squish dear Jupiter.

- 18 -

THiS TiME WHEN i OPENED MY eyes—or eye, I should say, because one of them was swollen shut—people who all looked sort of familiar were standing over me. A security guard, the angry wind chime vendor, and a bald cop whose arms were as thick as my legs, whose legs where thicker than my body and who reeked of too much aftershave. Detective Peech? What was he doing here?

There was also his partner, Ol' White Teeth, gripping Tiffani's arm.

"You . . . ?" I said to Detective Peech. It was all I could get out. I meant, "What are you doing here?" I meant, "How come every time I turn around, there you are?"

"We meet again," he said. This time he smiled a little, which made him look like my one uncle who's always up for a game of touch football. "Portland's a small town, and we're both on the same case." Then he winked at me.

Tiffani was sobbing, her cheeks smeared with mascara. The door to the hallway where I lay was propped open. Sounds from the mall drifted in. Someone hollered, "Give 'em room to work!" and more people—big guys in blue uniforms with soft voices—surged into the hallway. They wore those flesh-colored latex gloves that stink and creep me out. I felt blood in my mouth. My teeth hurt. My face hurt on the left side. Someone had folded up a sweater and tucked it under my head.

I asked someone where my ferret was. A pair of hands held him out for me to see. He was fine. His long body swung out from under the pair of hands. A thought drifted through my head: Ferrets really do look like tube socks.

Detective Peech was tapping out numbers on my Emergencies Only cell phone with his enormous thumb.

"I caught her going through my purse behind the counter," Tiffani shrieked. "It was behind the counter! She was getting away, and I told her to stop and she just kept going. I don't know why I'm in trouble. I was the one who caught the thief. She's the one who should be in trouble, not me. I work at Nordstrom!"

Tiffani blathered on while White Teeth went through her wallet.

I felt dizzy. The blood in my mouth was warm and sticky, thick as a milk shake. I closed my eyes for what seemed like a very long time, but it was only seconds.

"What are these?" White Teeth asked Tiffani.

"I'm calling a lawyer!" she shrieked. "You can't go through my purse."

"What is it?" said Detective Peech.

"We got ourselves a couple of driver's licenses here," said White Teeth. "One for a Tiffani Hollingsworth, which is our young lady here, and another for someone named Jordan Parrish, who, according to the picture, is also our young lady here."

I had no clue what any of this meant.

My eyes closed and stayed that way. I was still unconscious when Mark Clark showed up, no doubt wearing his Paid Assassin Look.

I missed the last week and three days of seventh grade. The Hazelnut excused me from having to do my Boston Tea Party report. Instead I was able to write a report on how I helped break the ring of identity thieves that had been plaguing our city. "Plaguing our city" were the Hazelnut's words, not mine.

When the police interrogated Tiffani, she told them

that she, Jordan, and Dwight had worked the checking-account-number-stealing scheme for almost a year. After Jordan told her she was quitting, Tiffani began stealing information from her Nordstrom customers. Flamboyant Toc, creepy as he sometimes pretended to be, was right. It was downright nefarious (which I found out means "infamous by way of being extremely wicked"; now I just need to find out what "infamous" means).

The Poor Old Grannies who shopped at Under the Covers preferred to write checks. Dwight would copy the numbers, then pass them on to Jordan, who would pass them on to Tiffani, whose cousin, a sophomore at Portland State named Carl Hollingsworth, worked part time at a check-printing place.

Pansy had been right: This is where Jordan had gotten the money for her cool leather jacket and camera phone. According to Tiffani, Jordan also wrote checks for Cash Only whenever possible, and that's how she made the down payment on her cute red Jetta.

It was all good. She and Tiffani planned to get an apartment after graduation. They went window shopping at Pottery Barn, where they picked out the cool new furniture they planned to buy. Jordan had talked about going to college, but Tiffani didn't see any need for a college education when they were already making more money per month than most adults they knew.

Then Jordan was awarded the Hightower Scholarship and started making plans to go to Stanford. She had her picture in the paper and an article about what a fine young woman she was because only fine young women were awarded the Hightower. She wanted out of their identity theft scheme. She started talking about how it was wrong, and that really got on Tiffani's nerves.

Tiffani and Jordan argued about it for months. But Jordan liked the money. So she'd still collect the eyeglass cases from Dwight, but then she'd cry that she didn't really want to do it anymore. And on and on it went. The day I went with Jordan to Under the Covers was supposed to be Jordan's last pickup. She'd put her foot down: no more.

Tiffani had known it was coming. She was furious. She knew it the day Jordan won the Hightower and was suddenly a fine young woman instead of the daughter of a single mom with two jobs. So, for reasons she couldn't really say, Tiffani got a fake driver's license with Jordan Parrish's name and information on it. She held on to it. She didn't know what she would do with it, but one day it would come in handy. One day, Jordan would be sorry she'd ditched her best friend for some snooty school in California.

Then, on Valentine's Day, Tiffani was caught shoplifting a scarf from Saks Fifth Avenue. That very day Jordan had yelled at her at lunch that she, Tiffani, needed to grow up and move on. It was the "moving on" part that got her. Tiffani showed the arresting officer her fake license with Jordan's name on it. It was reckless, she knew. She wasn't sure what sort of trouble this would lead to for Jordan, but she'd hoped it was something big, something that would make her feel she'd gotten her revenge. It was pure luck that the dumb police lost her mug shot.

On the afternoon Jordan was arrested, Tiffani smashed the taillight on Jordan's cute red Jetta while we were at Under the Covers, where Jordan was picking up an eyeglass case for the last time. When Jordan called Tiffani from the Portland Police Bureau with the news she'd been falsely arrested, Tiffani thought she was a pretty clever chick. According to Tiffani, in the statement she gave Detective Peech, her phone call to Emma Larson at the Hightower Scholarship office was sheer in-the-moment genius. She knew Jordan would come running back once she was stripped of the scholarship. She would have no choice.

The next morning, feeling optimistic, Tiffani dropped in at Under the Covers to see Dwight, to tell him she and Jordan would be back in business in a matter of days. She was giddy with the little trick she'd played on Jordan. She bragged about it to Dwight.

She described to Detective Peech the way Dwight had looked at her. He wore those ridiculous Harry Potter glasses, but behind them she could see the look of disgust in his eyes. He'd told her that he'd just been promoted to manager and that she and Jordan might be back in business, but he was not. It was over.

Then he said the thing that had probably cost him his life, that stealing your best friend's identity was something only a psycho would do and that if Tiffani knew what was good for her, she'd get her crazy self out of there and never come back.

It was too much. Dwight turned his head to straighten a pile of books, and when he turned back Tiffani whacked him on the side of the head with her suede platform clog, the same one she'd used to break my left cheekbone. Then she took all the money from the register, left the store, and, in another spur-of-the-moment decision, tucked the bills into the pocket of Clyde Bishop, who was sound asleep against the wall outside the store, cuddling with his three-legged dog.

I got this whole story from Mrs. Snowden, who was able to connect Tiffani's check-printing cousin Carl Hollingsworth to another, much larger gang of checking-account-number-stealing thieves.

To show her gratitude, Mrs. Snowden took Pansy and me out to lunch at a restaurant where the waiters open the napkins for you and lay them in your lap. I ordered a sandwich called a croque monsieur, which is a fancy name for a grilled ham-and-cheese sandwich.

"My question is," said Pansy, digging into her Caesar salad, "who was on the phone the day Jordan was picked up? You know, the call you answered that got this whole thing started?"

"It was Toc, just as I'd guessed. He'd been after her to hook up with him, but he wouldn't take no for an answer. They'd had a fight," I said. Quills had contributed that piece of the puzzle.

"But what'll happen to Jordan now?" I asked Mrs. Snowden, pulling the ham out of my croque monsieur and laying it on the side of my plate. Even though most of the swelling had gone down from my broken cheekbone, it still sometimes hurt to chew.

"They'll continue to investigate her involvement. Right now they have only Tiffani's word, which, given that she's just confessed to murder, isn't worth much."

I tried to call Jordan a few times, but she never returned my call. Charlie said I shouldn't feel bad, that her lawyer was probably telling her not to talk to me. But I did feel bad. Jordan was my favorite cousin, my idol who floated above life, an angel with her perfect hair. Until the day I was electrocuted and was somehow rewired to look past the outside of people—especially my own self—I thought a perfect outside meant a perfect inside. Now I'm thinking it's the other way around.

I still thought Jordan should get credit for deciding to get out of the scheme on her own, for realizing that it was wrong. Charlie thought the courts might make a deal with her in exchange for her testimony against Tiffani. But one thing was for sure: The Hightower, and her chance to go to Stanford, were gone.

"I'm doing a huge story on this whole thing for the school paper," said Pansy. "They also want to talk to me at the *Oregonian*." Pansy happily stuffed a huge piece of dressing-drenched lettuce into her mouth. She was the fastest eater I'd ever laid eyes on.

Kevin didn't come to the fancy restaurant lunch, but Mrs. Snowden gave me the little origami box he'd made that day at the water park. I hadn't realized it was for me.

Inside it said, "U R Cool."

It was almost a rebus, but not quite.

My brothers and I were sitting on the Cat Pee Couch watching—what else—*The Matrix*, when my mom called and said she was coming to town for the Rose Festival and to make sure my cheek was healing up all right.

I had already been to a regular doctor and a brain doctor and a plastic surgeon and the orthodontist. I had seen Dr. Lozano, who didn't know the effect my injury would have on the other "changes I'd sustained"—her words—from being electrocuted. I was a little worried I would go back to being the old self-conscious, self-loathing freak show freak Minerva Clark. Dr. Lozano said only time would tell.

I had been doted on by my brothers in a way that was nearly embarrassing. Dish duty had been immediately suspended. Mark Clark stayed home from work to make me every soft food you can think of: tapioca pudding and chocolate mousse, cheese soufflé and scrambled eggs. He tried out this really nasty recipe with pureed cauliflower, but he didn't make me eat it. He said it was in the interest of making sure I ate my vegetables.

Quills had gone to school every day and picked up my final homework assignments and my yearbook. He even sucked up a little to Ms. Kettle, who was on the verge of giving me a C in religion until Quills offered to give her son bass lessons.

Quills was extra embarrassingly nice since he admitted that he was the one who'd sent the death threat rebus. He didn't mean it to be a death threat, he claimed. He'd just wanted to scare me a little. Here's a big secret: Quills is the coolest brother, but he's also the biggest worry-wart. That, for a guy like Quills, is worse than coming from a family of champion square dancers.

Morgan was busy with finals, but he brought me

DVDs—even *Troy!*—and fresh ice and towels while I iced my cheek, which the doctor told me to do a few times a day. He talked to me kind of endlessly about a lot of Buddhist stuff, how virtuous deeds were a shelter, and all life was suffering, and blah blah blah. He meant well, but I couldn't keep track of most of it. The doctor had given me some fierce pain medicine that made me sleepy. Once, he told me a Buddhist joke.

Question: What did the Buddhist say to the hot dog vendor?

Answer: Make me one with everything!

I didn't get it.

Mark Clark hung up the phone and said, "Mom's bringing that guy with her, Rolando. Is he her boyfriend, or what?"

"I wish the answer was 'or what,'" said Morgan.

"The swami?" said Quills. "Pass the Vines, would you?" We were eating Red Vines, at my request. The box had fallen between the cushions.

"I think he's a yoga instructor," said Morgan.

"That'll go over big with Charlie," said Quills.

"Charlie?" said Mark Clark.

"He called the other day. Said he was going to be home on the weekend, too. They both said they wanted to see Jordan waving from her throne on the parade float."

"Do they know our perfect Jordan is on her way to the Big House?" asked Quills.

"What's the Big House?" I asked. "Our house is pretty big."

"It means jail, dummy." Morgan threw a licorice vine at me from the other side of the couch.

"Of course they don't know," I snorted.

Not one brother called me on my tone.

We were at the part where Morpheus asks Neo whether he wants the red pill, which leads to the truth, or the blue pill, which allows him to remain clueless. I snuggled up next to Mark Clark's shoulder.

I took my new cell phone from my pocket. It was no longer for Emergencies Only, and it had a cool faceplate with red flames. I punched in Reggie's number. He was still mad at me, but if I'd learned anything from living with all these boys, it was this: He'd get over it.